Pr:

M000033022

Published in the United States by Harvard Square
Editions

ISBN: 978-0-9895960-8-4

Harvard Square Editions web address:
www.harvardsquareeditions.org

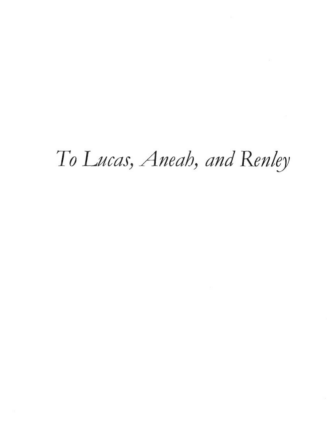

To Lucas, Aneah, and Renley

Part 1

The Election

1

'It's the genius of the American free enterprise system — to harness the extraordinary creativity and talent and industry of the American people with a system that is dedicated to creating tomorrow's

prosperity rather than trying to redistribute today's."
(Romney's acceptance speech at the Republican
Convention, August 30, 2012)

*   *   *

I first saw her one early August morning on Riverside Park. A hazy and humid morning when the only things moving were the few runners in their wet T-shirts, plugs in their ears, skinny wires snaking into a phone or an iPod in their shorts pockets. From where I lay, a bench where I spend my nights, I watched them, my eyes semi-closed, but they didn't see me: they ran looking straight ahead, without a smile, arms bent at the elbow, pumping up and down. As if they were really getting somewhere. Why would they look at a bum like me in his sleeping bag — a dirty pinkish-brown affair with a broken zipper and a hood-like thing I pulled over my head — with tears at the bottom, through which one of my feet stuck out?

She was startling because she looked at me and didn't immediately look away. A black ponytail dangled out of a Barnard cap. I kept my eyes half closed but I could see her just fine. I may be a crappy old tramp, but I can smell a beautiful woman any day.

Particularly since she wore only the briefest shorts on legs so long, slender, and lithe I could imagine putting a finger on the ankle and slowly, slowly going all the way up where it's warm and wet. Only in dreams did I see such scantily clad apparitions revealing so much skin and such full breasts.

She slowed down as she passed me, and I wondered why. I was probably an eyesore, or maybe she was just getting tired. And then she nodded. At someone else? I looked around but there was no one close. I began to smile, but she swallowed quickly and resumed her speed. Jogging fast now, she crossed Riverside Drive a block away at

113th, and I lost her. I felt an ache creep over me. Something about being a broken man, about dying, about things torn and diminished, about her golden skin. I thought I'd never see her again.

*   *   *

I passed the bum again. He evidently slept there. His big toe stuck out of the dirty sleeping bag — grimy with an ingrown toenail. He was facing the park, his knees bent close to his chest like a frightened child. A student in my Economics of Poverty class wrote a paper on the new wave of homelessness last semester. She had done a series of interviews, and her stories about regular women and children, old men, sick people who could have been your relatives living in the streets were devastating. I wondered what his story was.

I nodded as I passed him and thought he'd just smiled under his bushy beard, but I couldn't be sure. I did notice something else today, some black thing around his neck. It broke my concentration and I tripped on an empty plastic water bottle. Why couldn't people pick up their stupid garbage? I threw it into the trashcan a few feet away from the bum's bench. On closer examination, the black thing looked like a bow tie. I don't think it was one with a simple hook in the back, but the type you actually had to knot yourself. It wasn't a perfect knot. It was immaculate, however, and peeked out right from under the disheveled long and dirty hair, neither gray nor white nor brown, but a mix of the three.

Tucked under the bench were three bags. One huge blue plastic one, like an Ikea bag, packed full with a blanket on top. The other two were smaller, the canvas sort grocery stores sold you when you wanted neither plastic nor paper. They too were filled to the rim, and a bottle of water stuck out of one of them.

He disturbed me. Why couldn't he be somewhere else? Somewhere inside where I wouldn't have to see him everyday. His mere presence seemed to call for some action on my part, made me question whether I was the decent person I thought I was. I was decent. I felt sorry for him. But there were so many of these bums, most of them crazy out of their minds, or drunk, or they smelled terribly. They scared me. There were more of them now, even in this Upper West Side neighborhood. What could I do?

2

"Today more Americans wake up in poverty than ever before. Nearly one out of six Americans is living in poverty. Look around you...

"Our vision of an opportunity society stands in stark contrast to the current Administration's policies that expand entitlements and guarantees, create new public programs, and provide expensive

government bailouts. That road has created a culture of dependency, bloated government, and massive debt. Those policies have placed the federal government in the driver's seat, rather than relying on energetic and entrepreneurial Americans to rebuild the economy from the ground up. Excessive taxation and regulation impede economic development. Lowering taxes promotes substantial economic growth and reducing regulation encourages business formation and job creation."

(Romney's acceptance speech at the Republican Convention, August 30, 2012

*   *   *

I saw her again. I was drinking from my water bottle, sitting in the middle of the bench, my legs stretched in front of me. She walked past me, her black hair sticking out from the back of her cap.

You're back, I said, and she nodded. It's going to be hot, I continued in this desultory fashion, wondering what I could say to keep her here longer. Would you like a sip of my water?

She declined. Nice bow tie, she added.

I readjusted it. I like it loose, I said. Never could stand it squeezing my neck. I rummaged in my blue bag and pulled out an orange. Breakfast, I said. Want some?

Riverside Drive. Very convenient for me since I taught economics at Barnard and Columbia. Jake often grumbled about the commute to his Wall Street office but didn't talk about moving anywhere else. We got along fine. He was playful, he made me laugh, he was taller than I, and all my women friends were envious: single, straight, sexy, making money in New York, hey girl, what more could you want?

To say we didn't see eye-to-eye in politics would be a major understatement. I couldn't stand what I called his 'entitlement theories', and he had zero patience with my 'academic liberal shit'.

on the bench. He shrugged. Stay away from bums, he said.

You talk about them as if they were roaches, I said. He rolled his eyes, but didn't say 'here she goes again', which was all over his face.

"Romney picked Ryan," he said. I didn't respond. He thought I was your typical academic head, full of old liberal shit. He thought I didn't get debt and default and ignored the fact that America was in hock to China up to its eyeballs, and if the Chinese ever stopped buying American bonds, our economy would collapse. He was pissed at me because I refused to believe that the path to freedom was to cut government expenses and entitlement programs, and revive America with incentives for those willing to work hard and take risks. Read: lower taxes on the wealthy. He thought he did real work in his office on the Street, unlike me and the stupid paper I needed to finish and publish to get tenure at Barnard. But he made love to me like he couldn't get enough of me. Unlike most of the men I had met before, he was interested in giving pleasure, not just taking, and I forgot his tone, his know-it-all way of saying things as if he were talking to some dim-witted woman and I should just listen because he was right. But I knew deep down he didn't mean that, he knew I was smart, but he had fun coming across to me that way to rile me, and I wished he would cut the crap.

I fell in love with him at the Met Opera. We'd been in the same graduate econometrics lab at Michigan. He'd been so damned arrogant and competitive in that class, taking a perverse pleasure announcing he thought academic economists (like me) didn't know shit about what they were saying and wrote papers that predicted nothing. That wasn't for him. When I asked what was for him, he gave me his full Colgate-sparkling-white-teeth smile: he was going to make loads of money on Wall Street. I blew him off, having pegged him as one of these entitled silver-spoon wasp guys, and it hadn't occurred to me that he was having great fun playing to type and teasing me. So when he did call me after we reconnected at a Michigan alumni party in New York to say he had two tickets for Tristan and Isolde and would I like to go with him, I was so stunned that I said yes without thinking. His favorite opera of all times, he said. Turned out he had sung in choirs since middle school and was still taking private voice lessons. Math was a lot easier for him than music, he said, so he had gotten a Ph.D. in mathematical modeling. He sat transfixed during the whole opera, and when we walked out he said he would give his right arm and all the money he was making to sing like Domingo.

My best friend Abby, whom I had known since middle school, couldn't understand why I went out with him, and even less why it got serious. My dad, in his foot-in-the-mouth way, asked if it was the family money, because it sure wasn't his intellect. Of course, intellect for dad had to do with reading Greek and being fluent in at least four dead languages, preferably the ones he taught in the Yale Comparative Lit department — Greek, Latin, Aramaic and Sanskrit. He had read me Homer for bedtime stories. In Greek. I had loved it. He had been disappointed when I had gone into economics. My mother had died when I was four so I had no idea what she would have thought about Jake. My dad never spoke about her, as if he still couldn't bear to remember her.

I told Abby I had fallen in love with this big, funny guy because he drove an old Toyota and owned almost nothing besides a huge CD collection of operas; because he could be at once annoying and clever, turn from blustery to sweet on a dime, and was both easily pigeonholed and difficult to read. His inconsistencies put me off until I figured out what it was that consistently drove him. Cliché as it sounds, he believed in value added, and wanted more than anything to leave things better than he found them. She roared: that's why he works on Wall Street where they make nothing, just money with other people's money? That's the value added he's talking about? She couldn't stop laughing. I didn't tell her what a fantastic fuck he was, like making love wasn't just about him.

But there were also times when I wondered if I wasn't full of shit myself. Like last month in the seminar on the Economics of Poverty I taught in the Columbia summer adult education program. I had been going on about income inequality, redistribution, taxes, and one of my students, a bright woman from Topeka, Kansas, interrupted me and asked what could be done at a macro level that would make a real difference. She said she was getting irritated by the liberal kids who kept talking and talking about the one percent and the ninety-nine percent but had no idea what to do beside marching and chanting slogans and really doing squat, as she put it. Did they think that giving a dollar to a local bum on Broadway was enough? Or buying him a sandwich? Or even volunteering in soup kitchens? That changed nothing fundamentally. It was patching up, and it didn't change the chances of all the children who lived below the poverty level, who couldn't get out of the vicious cycle in which they were caught up by virtue of where they were born.

Several students had pounced on her at once. One woman had gotten up, red in the face. What do you mean, she shouted. I have spent tons of time in soup kitchens and maybe it doesn't solve the redistribution problem, maybe we'll never be Sweden, but at least some people who need it are getting food, including little kids who have done nothing to deserve going hungry. Just because we can't solve the whole problem at once doesn't mean we can't take action at the individual level. Not doing anything is one big fucking cop-out.

All right everyone, let's hear all the angles without shouting, I said.

One of the two men in the class talked about the merit of chanting slogans, because framing the problem in terms of the one percent and the ninety-nine percent had a simple immediacy and was getting people to notice inequalities they'd just as soon not think about. And that was something.

We had to cut the discussion short when the class ended. I had remained silent for most of it and felt badly. I, too, was all talk and no action. At least in politics, Jake was consistent with himself.

3

"This year's election is a chance to restore the proven values of the American free enterprise system. We offer our Republican vision of a free people using their God-given talents, combined with hard work, self-reliance, ethical conduct, and the pursuit of opportunity, to achieve great things for themselves and the greater community. Our vision of an

opportunity society stands in stark contrast to the current Administration's policies that expand entitlements and guarantees, create new public programs, and provide expensive government bailouts. That road has created a culture of dependency, bloated government, and massive debt." Preamble to the Republican Platform, 2012.

*   *   *

I stopped at Starbucks on Broadway before my run this morning and bought two coffees. When I got to the bench, there was no one there. The homeless man was gone. I had this terrible feeling of dread mixed with disappointment as I sat on his bench, which was still wet from the early morning dampness. Where did he go? Had someone hurt him? Someone maybe who tried to steal one of his bags and they got into a fight? Had a cop come and made him move on? What did I expect from him? Polite conversation? Another shared orange? I had gone nuts. What possessed me to stop at Starbucks and buy him coffee? So we would chat? And why should I be angry? Did I expect that after one short conversation, he should give me his forwarding address? The bench on 118th Street instead of 112th? But it wasn't anger I felt, it was more like grief, which was bizarre. What had I lost? There was nothing between me and the man.

I had mentioned him to Jake the other night. He had rolled his eyes.

You're such a damned do-gooder, he had said without smiling. You're full of stupid guilt and you don't know how to get rid of it. You're pathetic, you know. Why should you feel guilty for your education, your advanced degree? Am I so terrible because I don't torture myself about the money I make? You come from privilege too, Emma, with your super-educated father who has never said no to you about anything. Making money isn't a crime. I am not the bad guy, here.

Maybe he had a point. He loved to say he made money the old-fashioned American way, and he'd quote J. P. Getty's advice on how to get rich: "Get up early, work hard, and strike oil." Ha! Ha! I never laughed at the joke, and he said liberals had no fucking sense of humor.

Sometimes, I wondered why I stuck with him. But I was thirty-three and most of my friends, who weren't already married and with kids, complained about the men they met in New York: they were either gay, married, or didn't go much beyond a one-night stand. Jake didn't run around and was happy to come home. With him, I could relax. I was less anxious, and he had taught me to live in the moment and not plan, plan, plan. So what if we didn't agree about politics? He kept telling me he loved me because I was solid, predictable. I knew he hated surprises and didn't tolerate them from the members of his work team. He could live with mistakes if he knew about them, he told them, but surprise him and you were fired on the spot.

So you'd fire me if I surprised you? I asked him once, and he laughed and kissed me.

You won't, he said.

I hadn't bought coffee for the homeless man because of guilt. Maybe it was the irony of his sharing the orange with me. There was something about him that seemed gentle and reminded me of my father. But now he was gone and I felt like a fool. I threw the coffee in the trashcan and slowly made my way home. Before crossing Riverside Drive I looked North to check for cars and noticed a tall man stooping a little, a blue bag hanging from his left shoulder and two bags in his right hand, reaching the corner at 116th.

Jake was right, I was crazy to get involved with a lunatic. So should I go home and chalk it off to misplaced social guilt? But it wasn't misplaced. It wasn't all right that a human being had nowhere to go but the streets. If this wasn't my problem, then whose was it? I ran back to Starbucks. There was still not much of a line and I ordered the tallest latte, two large blueberry muffins, and grabbed sugar, napkins and a spoon. I hurried back up toward Columbia and finally found him sitting by the Alma Mater statue, his bags next to him. Campus security hadn't spotted him yet. I walked up the steps and handed him the brown bag.

He smiled. Hi, pretty runner, he said.

Do you mind if I sit with you, I asked.

Suit yourself, he said. Young women don't usually talk to me. I stink.

I sat down a few feet away from him. Have a bite. Security isn't going to let you sit here for long, you know, I said.

Yeah. I'll move, he said as he bit into a muffin.

* * *

Someone had left a New York Times in the trash. There was an article about Romney picking Ryan for VP. How was that for pandering to the ultra right to get elected. It might work for him. I wondered what these two thought about bums like me? Or did they not worry about us because we were only jetsam to be disposed of? But where? By whom? They couldn't arrest us unless we broke a law. I remembered waiting for a train at Penn Station when I was still giving concerts, and I had seen two police officers walk a bum away from the waiting area where he had been sitting quietly on the floor, his two bags next to him. I had asked them why they couldn't let him sit where it was warm, but instead were taking him outside where it was freezing.

It's the law, Sir, they had said. Just doing our job.

She hadn't been here all week. Maybe I scared her off. I gathered my bags and started going toward 116th Street, climbing the hill up to Broadway. I had to walk or my legs would start twitching again. I went through the Columbia gates and made my way toward the Low Library steps and sat under the statue of Alma Mater. And I saw her in her shorts and tight top running toward me, a brown bag in her hand and a grin on her face.

I saw you walking up Broadway, she said. Here, a latte from Starbucks and a couple of blueberry muffins.

Don't sit too close, I said, I stink.

Why don't you go to a shelter, she asked. They have showers.

Nope, I said, too many rules, lines for everything, and most of them are full anyway.

So what do you do when — when you need –

– You mean when I need to take a piss or shit?

Uh huh, she said and blushed.

The subway, if I can get to the 57th street station on the NQR lines. One of the few with a public toilet. Do you know, I told her, that there were 1676 public toilets in the NY subway in 1940 and only 28 of them now, half of them broken and the rest a stinking mess? If I can't get there, I go in the park. I try to wait until dark. I have the free green plastic bags, you know, like people with dogs. I pick up the shit and put it in a trashcan. Sometimes the church on 114th lets me use their toilet. I guess God doesn't like you to crap in the street. Not a lot of people worry about this, you know. You're the first one to ask.

4

"The Republican narrative is that all of us who amount to anything are completely self-made. One of our greatest Democratic chairmen, Bob Strauss, used to say that every politician wants you to believe he was born in a log cabin he built himself, but it ain't so.

"We Democrats think the country works better with a strong middle class, real opportunities for

poor people to work their way into it and a relentless focus on the future, with business and government working together to promote growth and broadly shared prosperity. We think we're all in this together is a better philosophy than you're on your own." Clinton's speech at the Democratic Convention, September 5, 2012

*   *   *

You know what, she said, why don't you come to my place and get a good shower. I'll fix us a real breakfast.

I looked at her like she was mad and shook my head. No lady, I can't do that.

For a second she looked relieved. Maybe the thought occurred to her I could be psychotic and she could end up robbed or dead. But then her face got sunny again.

I mean it, she said.

You're a nice woman, I said, thank you for the coffee.

We can do some laundry if you want, she added.

What for? I asked. It all gets dirty again fast. No. You go on your way, now. I got up and walked away. I couldn't become her project. I had nothing to give her except maybe the feeling she was doing a good thing. I wouldn't be used. But she ran after me.

Come to my apartment. It's safe, she said.

What about your boyfriend? Don't you have a boyfriend? Isn't he going to be upset, I asked.

Should he be? She said.

So I went.

*   *   *

The doorman didn't start his shift until four p.m. The lobby was empty and the elevator was there. I was relieved. For the first time, I smelled him. A foul and bitter smell. What possessed me to do this? He looked around when we got in the apartment.

Nice place, he said. You live here with your boyfriend, right?

Yes. We're engaged, I said.

He stood in the bathroom while I gathered one of my disposable razors, Jake's shaving cream, a new toothbrush, a towel, a washcloth, and Jake's white terrycloth robe. There, I said, there's shampoo and gel in the shower. Take your time. I was about to say that no one was coming, but I stopped myself.

Thank you, he said. Are you really going to make breakfast?

Yes, I said. Scrambled eggs, bacon, potatoes, muffins and coffee.

He grinned.

*   *   *

She had started a load of laundry while I showered, washed my hair, shaved, trimmed my beard, and combed my hair. When the dryer stopped, I wrapped myself in the robe and picked up all the clean clothes and got dressed. Then I folded my three shirts, four T-shirts, four pairs of socks, four pairs of boxers, two pairs of chinos, two pairs of corduroys, my two towels and two blankets. I smelled of the boyfriend's aftershave, my clothes smelled clean for the first time in months. She stared at me with a slight frown when I came out, as if to reassure herself I was the same man.

You look so much younger, she said, and she sounded surprised.

*   *   *

When I heard the water run, I imagined how horrified Jake would be if he knew. I could hear him: A complete stranger occupying *his* shower, using *his* robe? Did I want to be robbed, or raped, or killed? Had I gone berserk? But I wasn't afraid. In fact, I felt calm. He didn't look like he would hurt anyone. His eyes were kind and thoughtful. Like my father's. He was articulate. Of course, this could mean nothing, and he could be a serial killer. But I didn't believe that. He was just someone who had fallen on hard times, and reaching out to someone in need wasn't scary. What was frightening was the notion that homeless people weren't real people, just cockroaches to be disposed of. What the Nazis thought of the Jews. If you couldn't solve the problem at the macro level, it didn't absolve you from trying to help an individual. What was that phrase my father quoted so often? Some old Jewish proverb, something like "it's not up to you to finish the work, nor are you free not to pick it up."

I couldn't believe the transformation. Forty-five at most was my guess. His hair was combed and he had trimmed his beard. I was surprised at how few wrinkles he had. A youthful, handsome face. He kept his left hand in his pant pocket, but his right hand had long, lean fingers and clipped nails. We sat down and began eating. He asked if Jake was going to be upset.

Yes, I said.

Why, he asked.

Isn't it obvious, I said: I let a stranger into our home.

You mean a bum, he said.

No, a homeless person, I said, feeling like an idiot.

Your fiancé doesn't like homeless types, does he? What about you?

> Some of the homeless men I see in the streets scare me, I say. And I don't? He asked.

> Not right now, I said.

You should be scared, he said. You don't know if I am off my meds, you don't know that I won't get violent, you don't know zip about me.

Tell me then, I said. You can begin by telling me your name. Mine is Emma. Emma Blum.

No, I'm going, he said.

You can come back if you need a bathroom and a shower, I said.

You mean every morning? He asked.

Maybe not every morning, I said but —

How often should I be clean, he interrupted. Once a week? Once a month, every three days? See, it gets complicated, Emma. So lets leave it at that. Thanks for today. It was great. You've done a good

deed. I am grateful. Bye. And he was gone.
He had eaten only half of what I had put on
his plate.

5

"But when all is said and done, when you pick up that ballot to vote, you will face the clearest choice of any time in a generation...a choice between two different paths for America, a choice between two fundamentally different visions for the future...

"My grandparents were given the chance to go to college and buy their home — their own home and fulfill the basic bargain at the heart of America's

story, the promise that hard work will pay off, that responsibility will be rewarded, that everyone gets a fair shot and everyone does their fair share and everyone plays by the same rules, from Main Street to Wall Street to Washington ,DC." (Obama's acceptance speech at the Democratic Convention, September 6, 2012)

* * *

I wasn't coming back. She had problems with the boyfriend. It didn't matter that I dreamed about taking a shower with her.

* * *

I had been working on my paper all week. It was a study on temporal discounting: how the future was discounted in economic decision-making, making risk appear less than it really was. I had been applying the theory to the banking crisis of 2008 and my findings were robust. Jake dismissed them. He thought risk was precisely the business he was in and why he made a ton of well-deserved money. The less regulation and the more money he and people like him made the better. His justification: capital was what made the economy run, and banking was the mechanism to move it. It was all global now and he saw no problem except for regulators' interference. He didn't seem to remember the Savings and Loan debacle of 1989, only nine years after deregulation gave commercial banks the same capabilities as investment banks and let them off the hook from the 1933 Glass-Steagall Act, which separated commercial and investment banks. Savings and Loans went belly up. They had made far too many risky loans, and their capitalization requirements had been totally insufficient. That disaster cost taxpayers $124 billions and the S&Ls $29 billion. Just a hiccup, Jake told me, a few

people making bad decisions. It happened.
Cost of doing business.

6

"If you reject the notion that this nation's promise is reserved for the few, your voice must be heard in this election.

"If you reject the notion that our government is forever beholden to the highest bidder, you need to stand up in this election..." (Obama's acceptance

speech at the Democratic Convention, September 6, 2012)

*   *   *

Where's my robe? Jake asked.

In the dryer, I said.

Why did you wash it? It wasn't dirty, he said.

Actually, it was, I said. I had someone up here this morning who needed to wear it.

Jake looked confused. Who? Who was here?

The man who sleeps in the park, I said, bracing myself.

You mean the fucking bum, he said? He looked at me like I was demented. You had him come here, he yelled, and — fuck, I don't believe this. Are you nuts? Do you know how dangerous this is? A total stranger who's probably deranged? If you want to be a bleeding heart, why don't you just spend time in a soup kitchen. It's a hell of a lot safer. But for God's sake, don't bring these —

These what, Jake? Losers, vermin, moochers, crazies? He doesn't have a place to live. He doesn't have a place to take a dump and wash himself. Is it too much to ask that once in a while someone think of him as a man and not an abandoned dog? We actually do better with dogs. They sometimes get adopted.

And that's what you want: to adopt him? I didn't sign up for that. This isn't anything I remotely want to do, he shouted.

I'm not asking you to do anything, I said.

Oh, yes you are, Miss do-gooder of 2012. This is OUR apartment. We share it, we both pay the rent, the utilities, the cable, the works. That's our deal, right? I have a right to expect the place not to be invaded by strays, who stink and leave their grime behind. You have no right to do this on your own and use my robe, my robe, for Christ's sake.

Silence.

I cleaned up, Jake. There is no trace of him. I don't see why I can't help him once in a while, I said softly.

Oh, once in a while, now? So it's not a one-time thing. Jesus, this is crazy. I can't let you do that.

How are you going to stop me? I asked.

He got up from the couch. You can't be serious, he said, his mouth so tight I couldn't see his lips.

Funny how things hang in the balance when you least expect them to. A robe left in a dryer, an on-the-spot decision I didn't know I was prepared to make until there I was, helping a man, and here we were, Jake and I, fighting about rights, about my apartment or his, and whether he could tell me what to do. I didn't like his face. It had turned red and mean and grown-up, someone scarier than the bum, someone I didn't recognize, as if he wanted to shake me to get me to come to my senses, or rather to his senses. We had agreed we would never let our political views get in the way of the relationship, and difficult as it had been, we had managed it. So far.

Jake, I am serious. This man is not dangerous. He may not even be on the bench across the street anymore. But if he is, I want to be able to help him clean up once in a while and give him a hot meal. It's not a lot to ask, is it?

I can't let you do it, Emma, he said with a sigh. I can't let you bring strangers into our place. You don't see the danger but it is real.

What's real, I said, is your shameful disregard for those who are not as privileged as you. I can't believe you pay more attention to your mother's dog than to a poor man who has no place to go. That's disgusting. And it is actually my place. Barnard rents it to me not to you. You don't have to pay your half of the rent if you don't want to.

Look, Emma, you're going to have to choose between me and the bum, and it shouldn't be so difficult, right? Because if it is, I'm out of here.

I was stunned.

How could one shower and one breakfast weigh so much in your mind, I asked him.

Because it seems to weigh so much in yours, he replied.

But there is nothing personal between this man and me, I said.

That's not true, he said. I've watched you in the last weeks, and you seem obsessed by the man. If you don't see it, then you should talk to a shrink and figure out what's going on. But I'm not going to sit around and watch you make an ass of yourself. I'm going to Nantucket for the next couple of weeks and if you change your mind you can join me there. If not, I'll pick up my stuff when I come back.

*   *   *

I had a precise sense of her physical being, what she smelled like, what she would weigh in my arms. I had no idea what went on in her head. I had seen her a week or so ago, coming out of her building on the arm of the chubby boyfriend, nice enough face, good clothes, broad shoulders. Not the gravitas I expected she would go for. I was obsessed with her, how she spent her days, why she was not running in the morning any more, if he had made her see how reckless she had been with me.

*   *   *

No phone call, no text, no email. Silence. I couldn't get Jake's

face out my head: his rage and disgust.
Like something had suddenly bubbled up to
the surface he hadn't known was there.
Looking at me as if I had ambushed him. I
remembered his 'no surprises' policy at
work. So I guess that's what he did: he fired
me, packed a small bag of clothes and his
laptop, and he was gone. Maybe he was
thinking that I would come to my senses
and follow him to Nantucket. He didn't like
surprises, but I hated exit lines and
ultimatums: their poison stuck.

The night he left, I poured myself a
double scotch and, like a wound-up doll,
paced the apartment breathing harder and

harder with each step as if I were close to some finish line, until I flung open the door of his closet and started throwing his clothes into a couple of huge duffle bags — shirts, sweaters, shorts, socks, ties, T-shirts, sweatshirts, jackets, the robe he had left rumpled on the bathroom floor. I found an empty box for his few books and precious CDs and threw them in there helter-skelter, with a sadistic rage I didn't know I was capable of. So much for his painstaking organization of the CDs only he understood. I moved it all into a corner of the second bedroom we used for storing our bikes, my electronic keyboard, his old camping gear, out-of-season clothes, tools, my pile of *New Yorker*s I couldn't bring myself to throw away, the old TV. I was panting and sat on the floor with my nearly empty glass, shocked to see how little he had actually brought with him when he had moved in five years ago. Was that all he had invested in our common life? I sobbed, big hiccupping sobs, until I got up and put it all back into his closet, his dresser, and the bookcase in the living room, sorting the CDs as best I could. He didn't own much, true, but that didn't mean he hadn't cared about our life. I had actually loved that he didn't give a fig about fancy cars, Rolex watches, and tailor-made clothes. I had no idea what he did with all his money.

Wasn't all the fuss and bluster about the homeless always about pushing my buttons, getting a rise out of me so he could laugh at how predictable I was which is why he loved me so much, he said. So why the big blow up now about bums, about this bum?

7

"There are 47% of the people who will vote for the president no matter what. All right? There are 47% who are with him, who are dependent upon government, who believe they are victims, who believe that government has a responsibility to care for them, who believe they are entitled to health care, to food, to housing, to you-name-it...

"These are people who pay no income tax… So my job is not to worry about those people. I'll never convince them that they should take personal responsibility and care for their lives…

"We'll see – without actually doing anything – we'll actually get a boost in the economy." (Romney's speech given at a $50,000 a plate fund-raiser in May 2012, video made public by Mother Jones magazine on September 18 and quoted by Maureen Dowd in her New York Times column of September 19, 2012.)

*   *   *

She came by this morning and sat next to me. I was reading Coetzee's *Elizabeth Costello*. She looked tired and drawn. Did you read it? I asked.

No, she said.

I told her I had also read *Disgrace and Diary of a Bad year.* I loved both, I said. Right up there with Roth. I went fishing in my bag. Here, *The Human Stain,* my favorite.

She nodded. I didn't come to talk about books, she said. Jake and I had a fight. First time. I mean first serious fight.

How serious, I asked.

Like he is moving out, she said. She hid her face. I don't know, she said. I felt he always had my back, but he doesn't any more. He's pulled away. Like the way we've argued about this election. It was different four years ago. He didn't vote for Obama, but we could laugh about cancelling each other out. This time, he is so far out on the right I don't understand him anymore. I am the one with a Ph.D. in economics, and he talks to me as if I know nothing, understand nothing.

And he doesn't like bums, I said.

No, she said. I saw the tears running on her face. And I don't even know your name, she said.

Matt, I said. Matt Marciano. I used to be a pianist.

Part 2

Hurricane Sandy

8

"Governor Cuomo has declared a statewide state of emergency. Major carriers have cancelled flights into and out of JFK, LaGuardia and Newark-Liberty airports, and the Metro-North and Long island Rail Roads have suspended service.

The Tappan Zee Bridge is closed and so are the Brooklyn Battery Tunnel and Holland Tunnel. On Long Island, an evacuation has been ordered for South Shore including areas south of Sunrise Highway, north of Route 25A, and in elevation of less than 16 feet over sea level on the North Shore. In Suffolk County, mandatory evacuations have been ordered for residents of Fire Island and six towns." (Wikipedia)

* * *

She came Monday morning, right before Sandy hit. I watched her cross the street in her black slacks, black boots, black quilted jacket, and a white wool hat pulled all the way down over her ears to her eyes. She kept her hands in her pockets and her head down. She made me think of an upside down half note. There was hesitation and a slight wobbling in her step, as if her boots hurt or maybe she wasn't sure she should go where she was going. She perched on the bench next to me, ready to bolt at the first sign of something, but what? Her eyes were red and puffy.

The hurricane's coming, she said. What are you going to do? She was looking straight ahead at the oak tree in front of us.

I don't know. I guess I'll have to go to a shelter. Looks like it's going to be pretty bad, I said.

Pretty bad doesn't cover it, she said. It's going to be brutal. You can't stay here. The shelters are already full. Come to my place until it's over.

What about your boyfriend, I asked?

Gone, she said. She stopped and wiped her face with the back of her hand. I wanted to hold that hand but she looked so breakable I didn't dare touch her. I didn't ask why he left, I waited. We sat a while.

Wish I knew why, you know, causes and causes behind causes — hard to unravel, she finally whispered so faintly I almost missed it. She abruptly got up.

I don't want to think about it, not now. Come and let's sit out the storm. You'll be safe and warm. She turned her face to me and I saw tears rolling down her cheeks. I was about to say something but she put her gloved finger on my mouth. Don't even think it, she said. You're not responsible. You were just there.

She grabbed one of my bags. Come on, she said. It's getting cold.

9

News Bulletin: Hurricane Sandy has left the New Jersey coast and parts of Long Island and Lower Manhattan devastated. It will be months, maybe years, before those who lost everything can rebuild their lives and, for those who lost children, spouses, or parents in the catastrophic storm, life will never be the same.

*   *   *

Forget it, lady, I can't do that. The Riverside Church is taking people in, that's where I'm going, I said. But the words didn't make it out, they got stuck somewhere in my throat as I watched her bend down and lift one of my bags. Be careful, I wanted to say, thinking that foolishness like this would drive her and the boyfriend further apart and she didn't look ready for that. But truth was, it wasn't her I worried about. I was washed out, broken, useless to anybody, most of all to this vibrant woman, filled with good intentions, swimming in self-deception, believing that rescuing me had no real impact on the boyfriend, that she would patch it all up eventually. I could see, clear as the rays of foggy light peeking out of the trees, that there was more pain to come to me no matter how carefully I had insulated myself. I followed her anyway, leaning into the cutting wind that was whooshing through Riverside Drive telling us it was futile to fight.

*   *   *

What was in a name? Everything. Bum. I looked it up in the Oxford American Writer's Thesaurus (2nd Edition): "*(n) Idler, loafer, slacker, good-for-nothing, ne'er do well, layabout, lounger, skirter, loser. (v) 1) Loaf, lounge, idle, wander, drift, meander, dawdle, mooch, lollygag. 2) Beg, borrow, scrounge, cadge, sponge, mooch. Bum deal: crummy, rotten, pathetic, lousy, pitiful, bad, poor, second-rate, tinpot, third-rate, second-class, unsatisfactory, unacceptable, inadequate, dreadful, awful, terrible, deplorable, lamentable. See Tramp: Vagrant, vagabond, street person, hobo, homeless person, down-and-out, traveler, drifter, derelict, beggar, mendicant, bag-lady, bum."*

I checked further in the Webster's Third New International Dictionary: *"(v) To wander like a tramp, mooch, cadge. (n) 1) Loafer, vagrant, one who drinks heavily, from down on skid row. 2) Lazy, indolent, one inclined to sponge off others and avoid work. 3) Hobo, tramp. (adj) Of poor quality or nature, not good, invalid, inferior, sponging, cadging, in poor order, bad condition, in a state of depression."*

I laughed, remembering Romney's 47% gaffe, except it wasn't funny. Not a single word in these lists had a positive connotation except wander, meander, and traveler, although embedded as they were with the others, they sounded miserable too. And I felt shame that I was still thinking about the "bum on the bench" in spite of the fact that he had given me his name. Matt Marciano.

10

"In Manhattan, subway closed and residents in areas hit by hurricane Irene in 2011 were evacuated. More than 76 evacuation shelters were open around the city. The public schools were ordered closed and Mayor Bloomberg called for evacuation of Zone A, which comprises areas near coastlines or waterways. NYU Langone Medical Center cancelled all surgeries and medical procedures.

Additionally, one of its backup generators failed on October 29 prompting the evacuation of hundreds of patients including those from the hospital various intensive care units. US stock trading was suspended for October 29-30." (Wikipedia)

*   *   *

Can I call you Matt, she asked, I nodded. I couldn't remember when I had last heard someone say my name. My name is Emma, she said. I nodded again. She had told me before, but I didn't mention it. I stood there, my bags on the floor around me, staring at her face, the kind of face that revealed everything. All I could think was how dangerous her life had to be for her because she made herself so vulnerable. Right now, she looked scared, embarrassed, on the cusp of regretting she had asked me in. I should have bolted.

*   *   *

Look, I said, we'll get used to each other. You can sleep on the sofa bed in my study. You know where the small bath with the shower is: at the end of the hall. The washer and dryer are in the closet next to it. Use whatever you need. I don't know how long this will last, but you are welcome to stay until it's safe out there again.

I couldn't stop jabbering and all the time he kept looking at me as if he were memorizing me.

Thank you, he said. I will take a shower now.

He picked up his three bags and walked away. He looked taller. How could it possibly *ever* be safe for anyone out there?

He was gone a long time. I moved my computer to the bedroom and, because classes were cancelled, I sat down to get some work done while we still had power. Mostly to keep my mind off the fact that a complete stranger was in my apartment and I was alone with him. I could hear the wind picking up wildly, the branches on the trees frantically swishing around. I could see waves swelling on the Hudson, and I thought I should start putting hurricane tape on the windows. I was about to get up when my cell phone rang.

Are you all right? Jake asked.

Yeah, a lot of nasty wind but everything up here is fine so far. They say it's going to hit New Jersey and Long Island hard, I said. And you?

We're okay, he said, and then there was silence. He finally cleared his throat: "Well, take care of yourself," he said, and he hung up.

I kept looking at the phone in my hand, wondering why I was feeling I had just been caught cheating?

11

"Looking at photographs of the damage — overwhelming destruction that defeats the spirit just to look at it — I try to put myself in the place of the homeowner. I ask myself, as I have asked myself over and over and over again this past week, could I hold up in the face of such oppressive adversity, or would I simply drop to the floor, curl up into a little

ball, and quietly go mad?" David Bartlett, a reader from Keewenaw Bay, MI, responding online to the NY Times.com coverage of the hurricane, November 6, 2012

*   *   *

I struggled to push away the images of the shelters: water dribbling from miserly nozzles, lukewarm on good days, ice cold most of the time, always brownish. Rusty pipes, they said. Shit, I thought; fights with other dilapidated bodies who kept shoving, elbowing, jostling for your space, groping you if they could; gripping my soap tight so it wouldn't be stolen; rushing so I wouldn't have to lay myself bare anymore than

necessary to these yahoos who had been at
it far longer than I and didn't give a rat's ass
about me except I breathed their air and
there wasn't enough of it for everyone. I'd
hurry to get into my grungy clothes and the
hell out. Then.

I stayed and stayed in her shower, eyes
closed, luxuriating in the hot water, the
powerful stream pounding out the soreness
of my shoulders, penetrating crevasses,
sloughing off sweat, dirt, fatigue, flooding
the tiled floor, fogging up the shower door,
bouncing off a naked body I never looked at
anymore. I lingered, the faint vanilla scent of
the soap sticking to my skin, until, for the

first time in years, I felt a stirring in my loins and saw the face of a woman: a face with lines from pain that had firmly settled; a face I had devoured with my eyes, my mouth, my hands, hers shaking uncontrollably, then her head bobbing up and down and sideways, then her whole body trembling and limp, like a puppet the puppeteer allowed to sag and crumble. I could hardly breathe. Marcy. The last shower we took together, I held her up so tight against me so she wouldn't slip that I almost choked. I had rubbed her back with the glycerin soap she liked, covering her mouth with mine, feeling she was all I had, knowing time was cheating us faster and faster. There was nothing left for me when she was gone. I thought. And then I lost music.

Time messed with your mind, kept you the fool. The image fled as fast as it came.

The white terrycloth robe hanging on the bathroom door was the one I had used before: soft, thick, a size too large. I wondered whether he had left Emma for good or if he was just scaring some sense into her. I didn't use the robe.

*   *   *

You're not wearing your bow tie, I said. I handed him a large cup full of coffee with lots of milk and sugar. He was sitting at the kitchen table, bare-feet, in clean rumpled T-shirt and pants, and I could hear the washing machine whirring in the back. His hair curled around his face and was still dripping on his shoulders. He had shaved and trimmed his beard. He kept his left hand on his knees, but his right hand went up to his neck.

The bow tie's in my bag, he said.

Your father gave it to you, right? I asked. He said nothing. If you don't want to talk about it, I began, but he stopped me.

What's the point, he said. This isn't a date.

He stopped and looked at me with a smile that could hardly be called a smile, just a stretch of his lips, as if he didn't want to be rude or ungrateful. I wanted to tell him that I cared about what got him on the street, schlepping three bags full of dirty clothes, at the mercy of the wind and the rain, showering and drinking coffee in a stranger's home. But I was afraid. I didn't know how to ask without intruding or without sounding like a social worker. He didn't say more. He drank the rest of the coffee.

The dryer, he said. I need to put things in the dryer.

* * *

She was curious about me. But once you began talking you started something. We already had gone way farther than we should: I was using her toilet, washing my clothes, drinking her coffee, and if she had her way, I would sleep in her spare bed. And where would that get us? Into hers? After one night, two nights, three nights, I'd be going back on the street and she'd have to deal with the boyfriend. Back to the same shit. Didn't make any sense. I should have given her a fake name. I didn't want to tell her my fucking story so she could tell her friends. I wasn't interested in remembering. And I cared even less about the sympathy of a stranger. Because that's what she was, that's all she would ever be. And I should stop fantasizing.

*   *   *

I worked all day in my study, wondering every once in a while if I should go and talk with him, offer him food or coffee, something. But I didn't. I heard nothing. By late afternoon, I came out of hiding and found him sitting on the floor in the living room next to his clothes: one pile of wrinkled clean clothes, and a stack of neatly folded shirts and T-shirts. He was smoothing more clothes with his right hand, almost caressing them, then folding them with the minutia and care of a sales person in an upscale store. He only had a thumb and fourth finger on his left hand. He quickly moved the hand under the pile next to him that looked ready to be put away, lifted it, and placed the clothes with infinite care into one of his empty canvas bags. The other bag was already full. They smelled good, he said. He had washed the blankets and the sleeping bag too, he added and thanked me for letting him be here. He'd finish packing and he'd get going.

You can't leave now, the weather is getting worse and it's already dark, I said. Besides, it's time we make dinner.

Look, he began, I called the Riverside Church and they have a spot. I'll be fine there.

I sat on the floor cross-legged, facing him. Let's make a deal, I said. You stay here during this hurricane and I won't ask you any questions. You don't have to talk unless you want to.

Why are you doing this? He asked, a frown on his face. Why me? Most of those sleeping on street corners are lost crazies, he said.

You may be lost but I don't think you are crazy, I said. I don't know what made me say this, but once I did, it sounded true.

*   *   *

She will ask questions. She won't be able to resist. Shall I tell her that I followed her because I liked the way she moved her ass? I had not the slightest idea of what went on in her mind. All I knew is that it was my first hard-on in years, in spite of the fuzziness and ambiguity about what a man like me could expect from a woman like her, except more emptiness and shame.

*   *   *

Yours, he asked? He was fingering the CD's.

No, Jake's, my — I stopped. My what? Ex-boyfriend, former partner? Jake's, I repeated.

He nodded. Fine recordings, he said, all of them.

You told me your father gave you the bow tie for your first concert. When did you stop playing? I asked.

He looked up as if he had been touching something he shouldn't have, and pulled his hand back fast. I made it up about the bow tie, he said.

I didn't believe him. I've made some chicken and rice, I said, are you hungry?

Yes, he said.

*   *   *

We were sitting in the small kitchen and I wondered which one of them cooked. Did they take turns? Did one of them cook and the other clean up? Who shopped? Did they eat out much or ordered in? Whose territory was I invading? And why did she let me?

*   *   *

What did you put in the chicken? He asked. He hadn't touched the wine. His face was relaxed, a little flushed. Years off him. Maybe mid forties.

Onions, orange juice mixed with a little chicken broth, I said. It's better with a whole fresh chicken. You stuff it with the onions, and roast it, and half way through you add the juice to the drippings. You don't need broth. I must have sounded silly going on like this because he laughed and said he loved to cook.

Since when haven't you been able to cook? I asked. He winced and looked away.

Maybe we should stick to the bargain and not tell too many stories, he said to the wall. You think you learn about someone, he continued, but it's all illusion. So many ways to remember something and hundreds more ways to tell it. I'd be making it all up. I am here. I probably shouldn't. That's our truth for tonight. Isn't that enough?

He turned back to me and his face looked tired again, like my father's when he emerged from his study after hours of fighting with a translation, and he'd remove his glasses and rub the sides of his nose. Why shouldn't you be here, I wanted to ask him but didn't dare. I wasn't sure myself why I had invited him in. Maybe it had been the comment from the Topeka woman in class.

*   *   *

I was lying down on her sofa bed. I didn't open it and left her sheets and blanket folded in a pile on the chair. I was using my sleeping bag. I couldn't sleep, of course. It was too warm, too quiet, too dark. Deceptively safe.

I heard the phone and after the sixth ring her muffled voice answering it. I overheard her whispering at first, then she was louder, angrier. Her last words were distinct. "I won't." Then silence, followed by the sound of feet in the hallway and breathing by the door of the study. I lay still, not wanting her to come in, hoping desperately she would. Then she was gone. And I remembered my mother, standing by my bedroom door one night, after she and my father had had another fight, breathing heavily as if she had climbed steps too fast. I was afraid she would come in and I wouldn't know what to say. I was nine. She didn't come in. My father didn't leave, not then. He did later, after he gave me the bow tie.

*   *   *

Jake called last night. Just checking in, he said. Everything okay?

Yep, I said. Just fine. But I couldn't leave it alone. Matt, the homeless man, is here, I added.

He said nothing for a while, then: first names, now. What next? The keys to the apartment? You've lost your mind, Emma. You have to get him out. The Riverside Church will take him in.

I hung up. What point was I trying to make? That I can do what I want when I don't even know what I want? He's right. I have gone insane. I walked around the apartment for a while, half hoping Matt was up and would hear me and come out. But there was only silence.

*   *   *

I woke up with a hard on. Did I really think that a shower and a shave were all it took to be a man and not a reclamation project? I don't know what's wrong with the boyfriend that she kicked him out, but it's not my affair. So what if she uses me. I would rather be here than at the fucking church.

*　　*　　*

Good morning, I said, when he walked into the kitchen, wearing what he had on yesterday. His right hand was combing through his hair to no effect. The same gesture my father made every morning at breakfast. The two of us together: I made breakfast, he read the paper or some book covered with mystifying symbols.

I'm making scrambled eggs, I said. Coffee is ready. Please pour some for the two of us while I dry the bacon.

He nodded and, out of the blue: are you sure you don't want him back?

I thought we weren't going to ask each other questions, I mean real questions, I said.

We can, he said, we just don't have to answer them. I will leave, of course. I will leave anyway, he added almost as an afterthought.

It's not about you, I said.

He said nothing but I saw "then who?" in his eyes.

*   *   *

It got simple real fast when you lost everything. The trick was to want nothing. I had managed that pretty well. Until now.

*   *   *

Matt leaving would equal Jake coming back. Looked like a simple enough equation. But there were too many variables. Take Matt leaving: when? Today? Tomorrow? In a week? Because he decided to leave? Because I asked him to? Because I left the door open for him to come back? Or because I didn't? Take Jake coming back: because he wanted to? Because I wanted him to? Because he didn't ask me to throw Matt out? Coming back when Matt was still here? After he waited for Matt to go? Or coming back only to pick up his things?

*   *   *

You make a good breakfast, I said.

I am very experienced in breakfasts, she said.

How so? I inquired.

I was four when my mother died. My father hired a woman who came in the afternoons to clean, do laundry, shop, be there when I came home from school, and to prepare dinner for us. My father took care of breakfast at first, a euphemism for cereal or burnt toast. At seven, I got tired of the toasts and took over, first with plain scrambled eggs. In time, it got more elaborate.

Do you remember your mother, I asked.

Not really she said. I only have a fuzzy photograph of the two of us together on my fourth birthday. My father took it and he's never been very coordinated.

Didn't your father have pictures of her?

He didn't, she said. I looked when he wasn't around and found none and nothing that belonged to my mother. It's like he'd erased her. He never talked about her, not even when I asked him questions. Kind of like you, she added with a tight smile.

*   *   *

He reminded me of my father. For all the closeness we had, my father and I, the meals we had eaten together, the stories he had read to me at night, his insistence that I think for myself, and his encouragements in everything I attempted, I'd never been able to get close to the core of his grief. Maybe it was all he could do to stay alive for me. Kids had asked me why my mother didn't pick me up at school anymore and I told them the men had put her in a hole. The hole was real: deep, dark, and cold. Dead implied time in a way I couldn't grasp. For a long time I thought she was coming back. For a while, I could smell her carnation scent. And I remembered one scene: she was in front of a mirror, lifting her long blond hair and pinning it on top of her head, then yanking the pin and letting it cascade down, and I heard my father laugh. A musical laugh, like a little boy you tickle. What would my father say if he knew about Matt? That I was reckless? Kind? That life was never fair? That it should be lived anyway?

*   *   *

We are so righteous about our own pain, always sure we got more than our fair share.

As if there were scales to weigh it. But pain isn't like that. There's plenty of it to go around for everyone on the planet. It comes the moment we're yanked from the womb and it keeps coming.

*   *   *

The buzzer, shrieking and persistent, made me jump. It couldn't be Jake, he had a key. It was hard to make it out, but I finally recognized my father's voice on the intercom, unexpected. This wasn't like him: he never just showed up. He emerged from the elevator, bundled up in his quilted winter coat, ski hat, scarf, a small suitcase in his hand, an apologetic smile on his face.

I couldn't call, he said, my cell phone is dead and there is no power in New Haven and it won't be back for at least another week, maybe two. I thought I'd come here. A friend was driving to the city and dropped me off, and well, I hope it's okay.

I'm glad you're here, Dad, I said. I was worried about you. Jake's gone. To Nantucket.

Ah, my father said. Things okay there?

Apparently, I said.

Matt was standing in his socks in the living room when my father walked in.

Dad, I said, this is Matt Marciano, a friend. My dad, Saul Blum. They shook hands.

Marciano? My father said. I knew a pianist by that name. I mean, not personally, but I heard him play several times. Are you by chance related?

I'm sorry, he said, I have to get going.

No, please, no, I said, not exactly begging but close. My father looked at me, said nothing, struggled out of his coat, his shoulder clearly giving him pain, and handed it to me to hang in the closet.

There is no need to go, Matt, I said. Not now. We can easily manage. Dad, you'll sleep in my room and I'll take the couch.

*   *   *

I should have gone, of course. But it was wretched outside. I was a pianist, I said. I didn't think they heard me.

*   *   *

My father and I sat in the kitchen drinking coffee.

What do you know about him, I asked.

He smiled. I should be asking you, he said.

Nothing, I said. He's been sleeping on one of the benches across the street. I started talking to him a couple of months ago, when I run in the morning. He is educated, reads Coetzee and Roth, has a mangled left hand and owns a bow tie. That's pretty much all I know.

My father looked at me, the way he used to when I was little and he wanted me to know that, whatever it was I didn't want him to know, he knew and if I couldn't tell him just yet that was okay.

You used to bring strays home all the time, he said. Kittens and dogs, wounded birds, a kid from school his mother hadn't picked up. We kept some, always fewer than you wanted, we returned some, some we took to the animal shelter, and I had to console you for days. Jake's okay about it?

I shook my head.

Well, he said, this may not be entirely bad.

Why don't you like Jake? I asked.

Whether I like him or not isn't the point, Emma. I like him fine. I don't live with him.

Later, I asked him when he had heard Matt play.

A while back, he said. You were still in Michigan. He played the Diabeli Variations in Woolsey Hall. There was another time in New York, Beethoven's fifth concerto with the Philharmonic.

How on earth do you remember what he played? I asked.

I can still see the program, he said. He was better than anyone I had heard before. The crowd wouldn't let him go. I also heard him at Barge Music in Brooklyn, he went on. Susanah Goldberg drove me there.

Who's Susanah Goldberg? I asked.

A friend of your mother's, he said, looking rueful. I know, I should have told you. She lives in Boston and comes to New Haven every once in a while. She went to the New England Conservatory with your mother. They were both singers.

My mother was a singer? I blurted.

Yes, he said. She sang at the Met before you were born and until — until she died.

My God, Dad! What else don't I know about her? I don't even remember her, I can't put a face on her. Why? Why didn't you ever talk to me about her? Did you think I would forget her, like she was never there, so I would think she never died?

He looked grief stricken. I thought it'd be easier, he said. Obviously I was terribly wrong.

Easier for you or for me? I asked.

I thought for you, he hesitated — well, of course for me too. I couldn't, Emma, I was dying, and I was petrified that you might end up losing both of us.

So you kept nothing?

There is a box, he said. Letters, photos, programs, recordings, her jewelry.

Where? I looked everywhere in the house when I was nine. I wanted to know something about her, anything. I couldn't find a thing, as if she had never lived in the house, or just never lived. Like I had invented her. I was so scared to ask you, you know, I thought you'd get mad at me and think your love wasn't enough for me.

I keep it all at the bank, he said.

Do you ever go to look at her things, I asked.

On her birthday, he said. It never gets easier, in spite of what everyone tells you.

And what about me, I said. Am I supposed to wait until you die to know my mother?

* * *

There was an electronic keyboard in the storage room. A piece of crap. Never liked them. Marcy had one when I met her. Couldn't afford a real piano. I think she was in love with my Steinway much before she was in love with me, maybe even before I was in love with her. I gave it to Lucie, the little girl on the first floor, when I finally left my apartment. She'd been practicing on a beat up old upright her mom had dug up at a Salvation Army store in Brooklyn. It was never in tune. She'd come up after school when I was practicing, and sit quietly on the floor, her arms around her knees, her eyes closed. She'd never heard a grand piano. When I was done, she'd get up and caress it as you would a person you loved whom you didn't want to wake. I'd let her play on it. Even the scales were more fun, she'd say. She once asked me how much it cost to get a piano like that. When I told her, her face fell. Oh, she said, with such defeat in her voice. I gave her all my scores. She asked me if she was to keep them and the piano until I came back, and I told her I wasn't coming back, they were hers now. She looked at me, her face all scrunched up, her eyes pleading – you wouldn't be kidding me, would you? It's yours, Lucie, for real, I said. She jumped in my arms and kissed me,

then tore down the stairs shouting, *Maman,
Maman*, Matt gave me his piano.

*   *   *

The voices from the living room came
through muffled and I couldn't make out
the words, but I heard the beat. My father,
Matt, my father, Matt. Short sentences.
Then silence. Then moving noises: boxes
pulled across the floor, something falling,
laughter. Matt, I thought. And then I caught
something: let's put it there. My father. They
had brought something out of the storage
room.

I came out of my bedroom to look. My keyboard was on the dining room table and Matt was wiping it with a damp paper towel. My father was sitting on the sofa, his Cheshire grin on his face.

Do you know where the cord is, he asked?

With the earphones in a shoebox, I said. I'll get it. I came back with the keyboard stand and the box. Voila, I said.

So you play, Matt said.

Yeah, but I haven't since graduate school, I said. I was spoiled, you see: Dad has a glorious Steinway at home, so I never liked the keyboard. But when you live in cramped spaces with roommates, you have to have something that doesn't take room and doesn't make noise.

Your sheet music. Still have it? He asked.

I went back to the storage room and emerged with another box.

Here, I said. We watched him take out the books one by one, until he got to the thick Beethoven sonatas - the two volumes set.

Ah, he said. Which ones did you play?

The easy ones, I said.

None of them are easy, he said.

The Steinway was Emma's mother's, my father said, and turning to me, he added: it's yours whenever you want it, you know.

Where would I put it? I asked.

Is it a grand? Matt asked.

My father nodded.

You have room in the study, Matt said. Just move the desk under the window, against the wall.

You mean the piano in the middle of the room? I asked?

Yes, he said. That's where a grand should be so it can breathe.

*   *   *

This was going too fast. I didn't live here.

*   *   *

What happened to your hand, my father asked. Matt reflexively stuck the hand in his pocket and shook his head.

No stories, he said.

I'm sorry, my father said.

This wasn't like him. Not the sorry part, the questioning. He wasn't a nosy person. I am an old Brit, he'd say, meaning he was reserved, in control of his emotions, respected personal boundaries, words that when I was growing up set me on edge, like the screeching of chalk on a blackboard. And here he was, asking someone he had barely met intrusive questions. I said nothing. It was as if the cold wind had found its way into the apartment. Matt turned around and went into the study.

*   *   *

If I could explain, I would. To myself at least. But the boredom, lethargy, disuse, the silence day after day, had made my brain good only for small obsessions: tying the bow tie properly, packing the bags neatly, folding the blankets exactly right with no creases, thinking only about whacking off, like a pimpled adolescent. Lately, I saw her face, her pretty ass, and imagined fucking her. What would she say to that, my beautiful professor? And her father? Maybe Odysseus' banging away on his way home sounded better in Greek. If I could spin it in Greek my life might sound like a tale instead of a soap opera. *Tell me, O muse, of that ingenious hero who travelled far and wide after he had sacked the famous town of Troy.* I didn't sack anything. I was just a piano player who couldn't play anymore.

*   *   *

I've been on the street for three years, he said.

The three of us were sitting at the table with tuna sandwiches and beer.

I've explored the city for shelters and places friendly to the homeless. Some oxymoron, he sneered. No one wants you. They feel sorry for you but they want you to go to another street corner, preferably not in their neighborhood. And lots of crazies out there, sick people who don't know who they are, who are psychotic, demented, old and stinky, and they scare everyone. I watch them, the well-dressed folks who approach the bums: they scrunch up their noses just a little, you know, to sniff if they stink, then maybe they drop a few coins or hand them a buck, careful not to touch a hand or anything. And worse, all that pity in their eyes. Worse yet, you watch the bums play to their guilt.

Is that what you think? I said. That I feel guilty and took pity?

What else? He said. You are a compassionate woman, so you want to do something to help the poor slobs who sleep in the streets.

You have it wrong, I said. I don't want to do something for the poor slobs out there, or if I do, it's not by taking them to my house. So what is it then? He asked.

They were both looking at me and heat came up my shoulders and my face. I was silent for a minute.

It's — well, I saw something, I don't know what I mean, I said, but I didn't see a category, I saw a man, you know, under the grime and the clothes. And I liked that man. You. Is that so wrong?

And your boyfriend? He isn't real under the clothes? He asked.

Yes, he is, too. And I looked up. You tell me, I said with anger in my voice, why did *you* come? For a warm shower and a hot meal?

What the fuck else, he said.

I decided not to cry.

*   *   *

Why hurt her? Better leave. Now. Or I should tell her – what? That I liked her too, with her clothes on, and even more when I thought of her with them off? So lame. The way little boys talk, when they are too scared to use big words like love because they know nothing about that yet, and they don't want to sound like girls, and the crap they talk with the other boys is all about fucking and getting laid and having some and eating pussy. And they have no clue what it really means because none of them have done anything yet except they wake up and their sheet is wet. What was she scared of? Losing the boyfriend? No. She wouldn't have asked me again. The question was what was *I* afraid of. That my hand would repulse her, if not now, later?

12

Chris Christie on Sandy Aid: House Republicans were "Disappointing and Disgusting to Watch."

"There is only one group to blame for the continued suffering of these innocent victims: the House majority and their speaker, John Boehner," he said. "This is not a Republican or Democratic

issue. Natural disasters happen in red states and blue states and states with Democratic governors and Republican governors. We respond to innocent victims of natural disasters, not as Republicans or Democrats, but as Americans. Or at least we did until last night. Last night, politics was placed before oaths to serve our citizens. For me, it was disappointing and disgusting to watch." (Huff Post - Politics, posted on January 2, 2013)

* * *

I asked my father whose idea it had been to get the keyboard out. He and I were alone in the kitchen.

Matt's, he said. He'd seen it in the storage room and he wondered who played it and why it wasn't being used. I told him it was yours, and I didn't know when you had stopped playing. When did you?

When Jake moved in, I said. He was always listening to opera, I started enjoying it, and I never did like to play on the keyboard with the earphones. Felt too much like college again. There isn't enough time anyway, you know, work and things.

Shame, my father said, you were good and you enjoyed it. I never had to push you to practice.

I'll get back to it eventually, I said.

Matt could help, he said. I began shaking my head. Don't dismiss it so fast, he said.

Come on, Dad, he won't even talk about what happened to him. A famous pianist who loses his hand? It's a tragedy right? I can't ask him.

My father gave me a hard look. And being on the street is better? He asked. Because that's where he is going back to, you know. What else can he do? Live here with you? For how long? And what about Jake?

I didn't know what to say because I didn't know what to think. Had Jake really decided he wasn't coming back? Nothing was truly settled. I could still push the reset button. All I had to do was send Matt away, call Jake, apologize. And never invite bums in again.

Do you want him back, my father asked again.

I don't know, Dad, I said.

I think you do know, Emma, he said. But Matt isn't a pawn. He is a real person in your life now, because you invited him and he chose to come. You can't just disinvite him when it suits you. And if I may say what I really think, I don't believe Matt has much to do with how you feel about Jake and whether you should stay together.

* * *

I liked her father. Still teaching now and then, he told me, mostly grad students who worked on translations, still involved in all the controversies about the Dead Sea scrolls. When he told me his wife had sung at the Met before she died terribly young, and Emma was only four, I knew he understood. His voice was shaky.

I never recovered, he said. If it hadn't been for Emma — he let it hang there a moment — well I am here, he said with a small smile, and Emma is just like her mother: impulsive and kind-hearted, stubborn and very smart. I could never win with her any more than I could with her mother. Not when she had decided something. I take it you don't have children, he went on.

It wasn't even a question.

We tried, I said. But Marcy, my wife, was diagnosed and it all went very fast. I thought I was finished, but there were all these concerts I had agreed to do and for two years I kept an insane schedule. At least when I played I'd forget the pain and the rage. I lost the hand later.

*　　*　　*

It was an unfamiliar rhythm but it was a rhythm. My dad slept in my room. Matt convinced me to take the sofa bed in the study since I worked there anyway, and he slept in his sleeping bag on the living room couch. I made breakfast, prepared sandwiches for lunch, and cooked dinner. Matt cleaned up. We all watched the news on TV about the hurricane and the end of the campaign. We were mostly silent, coming and going out of different doors, sitting and getting up, crossing one another, carrying coffee, or tea, or a glass of water, a continuous ballet that reminded me of *Noises Off*, but with the sound muted. I was almost done with my paper, and my dad worked on his scrolls translation on the dining room table. Matt had moved the keyboard on its stand in a corner of the living room. He hadn't touched it otherwise. He read. He had found my pile of old New Yorkers and was going through them.

I hadn't heard from Jake. Not since I had hung up on him. The call came as I was printing the last section of my paper. His boss was flying him back in the company's helicopter. He'd made arrangements to stay at a friend's apartment. He'd pick up his stuff when the place he found was ready in a couple of days or so. Would that be all right.

So you've decided, I said.

No, he said, you have.

It didn't make it any easier.

*   *   *

She looked not so much tired as emptied.

I finished my paper. Let's celebrate, she said.

But her voice was distant, pale, if a voice had color, which it had. I asked about the paper.

Temporal discounting, she said.

I looked at her, puzzled. My face made her laugh.

It's the tendency of people to discount rewards that are far away in time. If you crave a cigarette, you'll give a higher value to one that's available now, than you will for a carton in three months.

Ah, I said. Isn't that obvious?

I suppose it is, but it does get more complex when you apply it to financial decision making, she said.

I didn't give a damn about complexities any more. Why economics? I asked.

I am good in math, she said, but not interested enough in the problems mathematicians want to solve. I want to do applied work that has an effect on policy decisions. Things like growth, taxation, education, investments.

And people pay attention to what you write? I mean people in government? I asked.

She smiled. I am just starting, you know. I don't even have tenure yet. Did you think people would pay money to hear you play when you were a boy?

Yes, I said. I was sure of it.

I used to be sure too, she said, and she got up, ran to the study, and slammed the door.

*   *   *

For Christ's sake, I shouted, when he came into the study, why do you tell me nothing? You don't think I am interested?

Well, I am. I sat on the sofa, my head in my hands, trying not to cry.

He sat next to me. This is about your boyfriend, right? He said.

It's over, I said. And I saw Jake, his air of ease and assurance, his tender voice in the morning, the private quality of his expression when he spoke to someone else on the phone. When he'd see me watching, his face would change, as if we two were together against the world. I wanted him back. I wanted to touch him, I wanted to feel his hands on me. And as fast as the feeling came, it went away. No. It was fear I was feeling. I saw myself looking like Leslie

Turner, a woman in my department, who was sixty-five and lived alone on Claremont Avenue with her cat and a yappy Schnauzer. She had the pallor of women whose skin had withered, who wore no make-up, and dressed in long beige skirts and loose colorless tops, sported long silver earrings, and wore comfortable shoes. I asked her once what she did in the evening. She watched the PBS News Hour, Netflix movies, read, ate a little more each year to pass the time and give herself some indulgence. Once in a while, she thought of coloring her hair, but quickly rejected the idea — what for?

*   *   *

I was back from a concert in Philly, I began. Late at night in Penn Station, in my tux and raincoat, and I was walking to the number one train to Brooklyn. There was no one on the platform but a homeless man sleeping on the ground against the wall. Then these three guys showed up, boys really, loud and drunk, or doped up, shouting 'fuck you motherfucker' every other word, and the ugly little shits started to strut towards the old man who wasn't even stirring. Hey, wake up motherfucker, this ain't a hotel, they yelled. I got pissed and started to lecture them. I'm not sure what I actually said, but something like, Leave the man alone, you little shits. Why don't you shove off? Take your antics somewhere else. Something very stupid like that. What's it to you, motherfucker, one of them said, and they turned to me. Leave the man alone, I said, or I'll call the police. They started laughing – the po-lice, they said, hear that? I'll show you po-lice, one of them said, and he pulled a gun from under his jacket and started shooting up in the air. Think they'll come now, he said, and he lowered the gun and kept shooting and I blacked out.

My God, she said.

I woke up at Mount Sinai, I went on. My hand was mangled, and I had a bullet in my left lung. I was lucky they said. The homeless man was dead. My wallet, with all of sixty bucks in it, was gone. The boys were never found. The bullets came from a semi-automatic weapon. Someone from the next train saw us lying on the platform and called 911. They fixed my hand as best they could. I was there for three months.

* * *

Hubris, that's what it was, he said. They wouldn't have killed the poor bastard, maybe kicked him a bit, then gone on if I had kept my mouth shut, he said .

I took his good hand. He looked at me.

Are you a romantic? He asked. Like my wife? She always looked at the bright side of love. But shame has no bright side, see. These three boys, they stick to me like skin.

Your wife, I said, what happened?

Parkinson's, he said, an unusual case because she was so young. She died a couple of years before the shooting. He pulled his hand back.

I didn't say anything. He got up and walked out.

*   *   *

I locked the bathroom and sat on the can. Now what? You tell your story and it knocks you out because each time it's a bit different, and you end up remembering versions of the story more than the events themselves. That's why I'd rather forget, I'd rather be numb. No more complexities, almost death. My debt to the old man who only wanted to sleep in the damned subway station so he wouldn't freeze his ass off.

Maybe he was better off dead. Maybe I would have been better off dead. I knew I was in trouble when I followed her. Big mistake. Big fucking mistake. Three years down the drain. And for what?

*   *   *

He came out carrying his three bags.

I am going he said.

Please, don't, I said.

There's no need to go now, my father said.

Then when? He said in a sharp tone. There is no good time, only in fairy tales. We make choices, and this is mine.

And just then, I heard a key in the door, and Jake walked in and stopped cold, taking in the scene: Matt and his bags, my father behind him, and me looking like I was ready to cry.

Well, he said, you have company.

I'm leaving, Matt said, If you'll excuse me, and he moved toward the door.

Not so fast, Jake said. Who the hell are you?

Jake, this is Matt, a friend, I said.

I didn't ask you, I asked him. His face was red, his mouth contorted into a grimace. He took off his cap and his coat.

I'm going, Matt said again. I won't be coming back. Let me through.

My father moved closer and stood between the two men.

Jake, he said, Matt is our friend. Did you come to collect your belongings?

Yeah, and not a moment too soon, I can see. And he walked past all of us, went into the bedroom, and slammed the door.

Matt, I began, but he was gone.

I felt it like a kick in my stomach, yet I had known he'd go. I went to the window and looked at the empty park across the street and the tree branches dancing wildly in a wind that whistled through the crack in the window, the one I could never close tight. I watched him come out of the building and walk away, his head down against the strong gusts. A woman passed him. She was walking fast carrying a grocery bag in one hand, holding a little boy's hand with the other, pulling him to make him keep up with her. The boy wore a red hat and held a soccer ball too big for him, and I caught myself hoping the ball wouldn't slip away and he would keep holding on tight to his mother. The way I should have held on to Matt, who kept walking, hanging on to his three bags that moved with the wind and bumped into his legs, and I could see part of his blanket half in, half out of one of them, a piece of black ribbon showing, and then he turned left and he was gone.

When I turned around, Jake was behind me. What the hell did you do to all my CDs? He asked in a voice so cold and controlled I hardly recognized it.

Oh, I am sorry about that — I began.

Fuck you, he said.

I heard my father clear his throat.

You aren't sorry, Jake went on. You have no idea what these CDs mean to me.

The time I have spent collecting and classifying them. Four hundred, Emma. And I know, I knew, where every one of them was. Am I supposed to be grateful you didn't throw them away? I'll come back later to pick up all the boxes.

*   *   *

How easy it was to flee. One foot in front of the other, thinking only of not letting go of the bags that flapped on my legs, their handles twisted tight on my hands, cutting the circulation. I felt nothing. Walk, I kept telling myself in my head, walk against the wind and the temptation to imagine life. Because if I did, if I let the fantasy take over, I'd end up thinking about what life could have been, and there lay the road to madness. So I kept walking.

*   *   *

We had been quiet all day. I pretended to work. Jake came back in the afternoon with a man to help him load his stuff into a van. We didn't talk to each other. He made a show of giving me the keys back, and his face at that moment looked more tight and sad than angry. I wanted to hug him goodbye, but didn't.

Goodbye, then, he said.

I nodded. I am sorry, I said.

Me too. And he walked out.

My father seemed untroubled, immersing himself in the papers spread on the dining room table, a hint of a smile on his lips. Aristophanes, he had said. I was glad for his presence. I felt fourteen again, when I had come back from summer camp. I had been kissed for the first time, but not by the boy I was pining for. The one I was in love with was sixteen, literate, funny, handsome to boot. The problem was his vulgar and stupid girlfriend: sixteen and big boobs. He and I took long walks together, talking about Baudelaire and Yeats, Bach and the Beethoven quartets, and I kept hoping that he would see how much smarter I was, ditch the other girl, and kiss me properly, not understanding that a brainy and still flat-chested fourteen year-old was no match for an older girl willing to "put out," as we said then. I came home, crying all the way from upstate New York to New Haven, and my father, who had no clue why I was in such a state, had simply hugged me and said I could cry as much as I wanted but when I was ready,

I should wash my face and we would go out to dinner. And I had felt at once good to be home.

My father brought Matt up first. He is an embattled man, he said.

What do you mean, I asked.

He doesn't want to be Matt Marciano, he wants to be a homeless man because just staying alive is a full time job, and he gets caught up in the mechanics of survival. But you keep intruding and he can see the old Matt peeking out from under the bags. He has nothing to offer you, just a broken soul. And he isn't ready to mend it. So he runs.

What should I do? I asked him.

He frowned. You know better than to ask me, he said. But for what it's worth, Matt knows where to find you if he wants to come back. You have unfinished business too. It is wise to think you cannot use each other to get this done.

I kept ruminating in my study, getting nothing done, occasionally staring at the street down below.

Late that night the phone rang. Jake.

I'm sorry it ended that way, he said.

What way? I asked

You know, because of a bum, he said.

It's not because of a bum, Jake. It's not about Matt. It's a lot of things.

I had no idea you weren't happy. You had me fooled, he said.

I didn't mean to. I fooled myself too.

Well, then I guess that explains everything, right?

His tone pissed me off. Forget it, I said.

Fine. And he hung up.

Unfinished business my father had said. Was that it? If so, how should we finish it? It seemed so abrupt. But the reality was that my feelings about Jake, about us, had trickled out. Not a dam break, but a slow leak. Could we patch the hole, paint it over, and make nice again? Earlier, we had talked about having a child, not just then, but later. Not because I really wanted to wait, although that is what I told him at the time, but because I couldn't quite imagine Jake as the father of my child. Maybe I should have trusted him.   Or maybe I had known all along that I wouldn't miss him.

Part 3

The Concert

14

Sacha Davidov leads two Juilliard Orchestra concerts. He conducts works by Adams, Barber, Ives, and R. Strauss on Friday, November 15, 2013 and leads the Juilliard annual student and faculty composers' concert featuring four world-premiere works on Friday, February 14, 2014. Both concerts are at 8 PM in Alice Tully Hall.

*   *   *

So that's the way it is with Lucie. A fight with a mother who doesn't understand. Every night the same – stop Lucie it's time. Time for what. She doesn't want to sleep, she's keyed up, ha! ha! keys, piano, Matt, Mr. Marciano she calls him, but he is Matt to her. He who wants her to practice and play and play some more until each hand moves on its own, the left and the right unconnected to each other, until she feels she doesn't control them anymore except it's all control, and he's now gotten her into the *Etude Révolutionaire*, a piece too big for her and for her hands, but he insists Lucie can do it, and when he shows her how with his one hand, he flies up and down the keyboard, the right hand first, then the left hand with his right hand. He's never told her how he lost the fingers in his left hand and she's not asking. He's very busy now, he's shaved his beard, looks like he used to, except happier, especially since he started teaching at Juilliard again, but that's not what's important, she doesn't give a hoot about that. Lucie knows she is only a girl, a fourteen year-old girl, tall and thin, with lots of curly black hair, freckles on her nose and cheeks, and big blue eyes, which her mother says she got from her grandfather, and she always adds: the only good thing about him, and all Matt, Mr. Marciano, wants from her is perfect scales, perfect arpeggios, and to feel when she plays. Feelings. She's got lots of those. So many, so new, she can't even start telling herself about them, and least of all her mother who's only worried about the noise at night and the neighbors. To hell with the neighbors and the stupid rules about quiet after nine pm. She's got to get ready for her live audition at the La Guardia High School for Music and Art and

Performing Arts. And Matt, Mr. Marciano, sorry, says she can do it. He said she has to get the *Etude* into her fingers and her head. Head's not the problem. She gets it, Lucie does. The anger, the passion, the pride, the desperation to be free. She gets that. She wants to fly too. It's her fingers that don't always follow, and she does scales for hours, exercises until her fingers are numb and she aches all over. He taught her to sit, to keep her arms loose, to stretch the muscles in her hands and her arm. But mostly he teaches her to relax. His voice does it, like he hypnotizes her, the deep voice, his way of looking at her, like he really cares, and she turns into a rag doll.

Of course Lucie is in love with him. He doesn't know it, she won't tell him, ever. He can't love her back, not that way, he is too old, she's too young, and her mother would have a fit, because she thinks Lucie is still a little girl. Her baby. And there is the story of the piano. How he gave it to Lucie when she was ten, and her mother was apoplectic, they couldn't possibly afford it – it's a gift, Lucie said, but her mother would have none of it and when she went upstairs to speak her mind to Mr. Marciano, he was gone and he had left nothing of his in the apartment except the sheet music in a box and the piano with a note on it that said "For Lucie, with great affection and good wishes" and her mother had to ask several neighbors to help get it downstairs. That's when she started taking lessons and working hard, and she kept hoping Mr. Marciano would come back even if she had to give the piano back, but he hadn't and they hadn't heard from him until last year when he showed up one day, and he looked so old and sick, and he said he had no place to go and could they have him for a while until he got back on his feet and he'd be happy to give Lucie lessons in return, and her mother didn't even hesitate, didn't ask him anything and showed him the little room in the back of the kitchen that was like a big closet, just enough room for a cot and a chair. That's all he needed, he said, it was generous and kind of them to have him, and he would never forget. And so he was back in their life, but Lucie felt the piano was something that stood between them, something that embarrassed her now because she had it and he had nothing, and she was afraid he would hate her and regret that he'd given it to her, and just like that on the first day Lucie almost bumped into him when he came out of the little room but they didn't crash into each other, he was just lost in his head and he didn't see her running in the narrow hallway, but they stopped just short of touching, and he said when do you want to start Lucie, and she said right now please. And they sat at the piano and he said she should play what she liked. And she played for a long time everything she knew, and he didn't stop her, he just sat there, his head leaning a bit toward her, his hands on his knees, his foot beating the beat, and it had been such a long time since she had seen him and she wanted to tell him she loved him, because she did, because she felt it in her hands, and they were moving faster than ever and she wasn't missing too many notes, and it didn't matter if she did because he said nothing, just listened and smiled, his sweet, kind smile, the smile that made Lucie feel hot all over, and turned her neck red, and she was feeling all funny inside, and when she felt like that she knew something important was going on, something that changed everything, and she played the best she had ever played.

* * *

The audition at the La Guardia High School was in a month. Matt, Mr. Marciano, said Lucie should go there for two years, and then audition for the Juilliard Pre College Program. Lucie's mother wasn't so sure. It was a long commute to Lincoln Center, and wouldn't her academics suffer with all the hours spent on music, and it was such a hard career, yak, yak, yak.

Matt never loses his temper, not like Lucie who stomps her feet and says it's her life and music is what she wants, and she doesn't care what her mother wants, and her mother tells her to stop acting like a baby having a tantrum, decisions like that are important, and Lucie's too young to know what's good for her and Lucie hates her mother when she talks like that, when she's afraid of everything and worries all the time, when she makes her feel guilty for wanting something different, something her mother never had because she had to start everything over when she came to America, and the more she lectures, the less Lucie wants to listen and she gets exhausted about her mother's prejudices and clichés, like they were the truth and should drive her life too – you'll see, you'll understand when you're older, and you'll thank me. Well, thank you but no thanks, and Lucie can't wait to go somewhere else, to a high school where she can finally do all day or most of the day what she loves most, and Matt, Mr. Marciano, is with her on that, and thank God he came back. He'll talk sense into her mother because she trusts him. She pesters him for advice, too much if you ask Lucie, bothering him like that for nothing, asking, is fish really good for the brain and how many times a week should they have some and lame stuff like that. Matt, Mr. Marciano, is so patient. Maybe Lucie will never get in Juilliard, but what if she does, and what if she becomes a great pianist, and her mother will be proud then, and – and – and she knows she's dreaming and what are the chances this really would happen, and maybe her mother is right after all and she ought to finish high school first, but when she thinks about three more years of total boredom with kids who don't give a damn about what the teachers are trying to teach them and who care only about texting their friends and twitting and posting on Facebook and stealing small things in stores, and smoking pot and getting wasted and screwing around with everyone and their parents don't even have a clue what's going on, she'd rather be doing scales and exercises and learn the damn *Etude Révolutionaire* and be part of some revolution herself.

* * *

She does have a friend, Lucie does. A girl. They met the first day of middle school. The boys in her class are losers. They're all about baseball or basketball – the players, the coaches, the teams, the scores, even the puny ones who couldn't score two points if they tried. And sex of course, which they are too young for, so it's all talk for most of them – who got some, with whom, how, who gives head and who doesn't, and her mother would be horrified if she knew. But she doesn't tell her. Besides, there is nothing to tell, she isn't about to go with any of the jerks, and they don't even talk to her. They call her The Bitch, they say she thinks she's better than everyone. She doesn't care what they think, what anybody thinks. Except Matt of course. But it's different with Matt because he doesn't make Lucie feel that what he thinks is how she should think, he talks to her like she's a real person with a mind of her own.

Lucie's girl friend, Nita, they couldn't be more different the two of them. Lucie was born in France, in Nantes, Nita in Brooklyn. Lucie has bushy black hair all curly and thick, Nita has black hair too but hers is long and smooth and straight and bouncy like in the shampoo commercials; Lucie is tall, Nita very short. Lucie is quiet and reflective, a bit shy, likes to be left alone, except when she plays the piano and she wants Matt, Mr. Marciano, to notice, Nita is forever in trouble shooting her foul mouth off, making brilliant speeches about inequality, the environment, smoking, and going to all the marches, and she skipped school for days to sit with the Occupying Wall Street people, and her parents didn't even notice. Lucie's the only one with a mother who sticks to her like fly paper and seems to know everything she is doing, Nita spends nights out and no one asks her where she's been. They are best friends, Nita says, and when Lucie asks her what that really means, she says they have each other's back. First time Lucie has heard the expression, have someone's back. You mean, I don't tell your parents where you are if they ask, Lucie asks. Yeah, that's part of it Nita says, and we also don't trash each other with the other kids, we're private the two of us, see, Nita goes on, our world of two. That seems a little silly to Lucie, like elementary school crushes, because in her head, she doesn't feel that close to Nita, she likes her all right and she will never tell on her or trash her, but she doesn't feel Nita is part of her real inside world. She never told her about Matt, for example, about the lessons, about the piano he gave her, about loving him so much she could explode. She can see already that Nita will eventually drop from Lucie's life, be like a souvenir, a name that will conjure up being twelve and thirteen and fourteen but who wants to be these ages again. They are best forgotten best stored away and it's better to think ahead not back. Anyway, that's the way Lucie thinks.

Nantes was a rainy city, an unhappy place, her mother told her when Lucie kept asking but her mother was always reluctant to talk about her life there. Once, Lucie cried and cried and asked why her mother wouldn't tell her anything: didn't she have a childhood? Didn't Lucie have grandparents, a father even? And Simone finally spilled it all out – she had been a high school English teacher, single, still living with her parents at thirty-five, her father a respected lawyer and a city councilman with a bit of a paunch and political aspirations and family money going back generations, her mother immersed in charity work, *des gens bien-pensants,* meaning conformists, uptight, minding what other people thought, leaning right with a touch

of xenophobia, not enough to vote Le Pen
but close. They were outraged when Simone
became pregnant and found out that Lucie's
father was the math teacher, a married man
with two teenage children, who managed to
get himself transferred to Paris and Simone
never heard from him again. She suspected
her father had had something to do with it.
They were relieved when a year after Lucie
was born Simone decided to move to
Brooklyn where a cousin of her father had
an accounting practice and agreed to
sponsor her and hire her as a secretary in
the firm.   She was now the business
manager, had a green card and had applied

for citizenship. She never went back to Nantes, not even for her grandmother's funeral, a dried up woman who only wore black and gray clothes and a perpetual frown, and kept the corners of her mouth down, congealed in a malcontent expression, her mother told her. The only good thing there had been having Lucie. And Lucie's grandparents hadn't bothered to visit them, not once.

15

Matt thought about Meursault, what it meant to be alone like him in Oran. Maybe all stories began with a brutal stop, a kind of hiccup that upended the world, emptied it, until you were face to face to no one, it was only you and utter solitude, and it became easier, little by little to sever ties, here and there, this one and that one. Sure at first, when he lost his fingers, some friends kept stopping by to find out how he was. He was too grim, too much into himself, he looked worse and worse, because he didn't care much about how he looked, as it if mattered anymore, as if anyone cared, and he least of all. Some friends lectured him, even got mad and told him to take a hold of himself for God's sake, get up, take a shower, move, react. They said things like sure you lost your hand but you could have been killed, and they didn't get it that playing was all that had kept him from insanity, from feeling the torture of losing Marcy. He didn't tell them of course because they thought that by now he should be healed, that pain eventually faded away, it had been two years already and it was enough grieving, get over it. And they began to space their visits, because they were pissed at him for being so stubborn and refusing help from them, from anyone, it wasn't normal this – this – they didn't know what to call it, and if they did they didn't want to name it, and maybe he should see a shrink, they knew someone really good, if he needed money they could help for a while, what were friends for, they really cared, anyway that's the way they wanted to see themselves and that was fine with him except he didn't want anything anymore, and he knew he was scaring them out of their   mind, because when they saw him they thought here by the grace of God go I and they were terrified, and he saw that their solicitude was a cover, a kind of down payment to ward off bad luck, and finally they were so frustrated with him they gave up and told him to go hang in hell, and he wanted to laugh because he was already there, settled in for the duration, the anguish and pain forever, his punishment for something but had no clue what it was he had done that deserved that. But of course there was no justice, it wasn't about justice, was it, it was about nothing, just random shit, right? Because he didn't believe, not in fate, not in God, just in randomness and now that he was so deep into it, it wasn't just a pleasant dinner conversation with sophisticated intellectuals anymore, it wasn't about Kant or Camus or Sartre or anyone and he was really seeing for the first time what random meant. How cause and effect worked in a random world. Ha! He hadn't thought it would hurt that much. He hadn't fucking planned it that way. But what did planning mean in a random universe, you, little speck of nothing whirling around billions of other little nothings? Answer that now, you little shit who thought you were so damn special, so gifted, so entitled to the munificence of the gods you felt so free not to believe in. Ha, tell me now. And the few friends left who still bothered to come, they looked so sad to see him "like that." And what did that mean "like that?" Like a poor schmuck, a slob, a lost soul, a madman, like a bum? No more solicitude, please. So he packed what he could carry, three bags, threw the rest out, except for the piano. Lucie was the only one who just sat there with him, said nothing and just took his good hand once in a while and smiled and her face lit up as if she understood. Of course she understood nothing but at some level she understood best, enough to feel something that moved her closer to him, that made her want to touch him, that told her words were not needed, words that she didn't know yet, wouldn't understand, how could she, but she knew they in fact would fall flat and come between them, so she sat there, her little face watching his, and she smiled and looked so healthy and beautiful and so much what a little girl ought to be like, free still, free to choose and hope and there was still time to postpone pain. So he gave her the piano. Walking is what he wanted to do, walking until his muscles got sore and sorer, until he got fatigued to the core, and lost, mostly lost. He wanted to recognize nothing. He left with his three bags, walked all day, every day, slept on benches at night, it was summer, so he didn't have to deal with the cold that can freeze you to death. Not yet. The heat wasn't kind either, he could sweat so much he was drenched and could hardly breath. He saved his money for water for the times he couldn't find a water fountain to refill his bottle, he held his pee and the rest of it for long periods at a time, he was wary of everyone, there were some who still had less than he and wouldn't hesitate to kill him, and he wasn't quite ready to die that way. In fact, what became clearer after a while, and the joke was on him, was that he had never been ready to die.

He had access to cash with the one card he kept well hidden, and while his savings weren't much they were enough, so he was never a real bum. He never had nothing. He could always eat something. He didn't have to beg. He didn't want to know what that felt, to beg. He wasn't investigating anything, He wasn't writing a book about the homeless, and doing field research. He wasn't Barbara Ehrenreich, who wrote *Nickled and Dimed*. A fantastic book, but that's not what he was doing. So what was it he was doing hiding in plain view? Trying not to think, trying to make himself as uncomfortable as he could so that just surviving without a roof over his head in the great city of New York kept him busy. He didn't want to befriend anyone, the other bums, he didn't want to feel their pain, he had enough with his. This wasn't an experiment. He wasn't testing himself, at least he didn't think so, not at first. He walked in pretty much every street of Manhattan. A slow paced marathon of sort. Until he had enough and started coming back to places he liked best, like Riverside

Park. He liked to look at the Hudson from every one of its bridges, the colors of the setting sun of course, the shimmering in the early morning, the stuff poetry and music are made from. And that's when he started writing his notes. Music notes. He bought a music notebook, and he began to hear in his head the sounds of the city, the cacophony, the cars, the sirens, the wind blowing in the trees, the birds chirping, the buzz of the voices, the silence at dawn, the rings of cell phones, the laughter and cries of children in the small play areas that dotted the park, the snoring of the bums who spent the night on a nearby bench like him. And the more he played with the notes in his head, the more he forgot what he was doing here, he just kept writing. *Fugue for the Right Hand*, he called it, for piano and orchestra. How was that for hubris. That's when he finally understood that he had never been a bum, not for a minute in the three years he had slept on benches. He wasn't crazy out of his mind, he wasn't poor to the core, he wasn't completely alone in the world, sick, drunk, addicted, or helpless. He had music, he had an education, a way of thinking about life that made him acutely aware that actions had consequences and that freedom to choose, while sometimes curbed by circumstances out of our control, was there if we wanted to exercise it. And that to refuse to do so was a slap in the face of all those who had come before us and left a legacy, some of it good, some bad, some indifferent, but marks nonetheless that kept us inching along. And he remembered his father telling him to stop whining, straighten up and pull up his socks. And that's when he met Emma.

He wouldn't have noticed her except as just another one of the runners in the park whom he watched for the fun of seeing their earnestness. But he was ready to see that she was something else altogether.

16

Last year my father gave me all of my mother's recordings which I downloaded into my iPod to listen to when I ran. Her Mimi, her Violetta, her Cio Cio San, her Marschallin, her Tosca. My mother had a beautiful coloratura soprano voice with a breathtaking range. My father was always the one putting me to bed, but I remembered now when she sang me parts of the *Cantaloube* songs the evenings she was home. They still haunted me. I stopped cold when I came to them in full for the first time in my iPod on a run. I had to sit down my head on my knees and someone came by and asked if I wasn't feeling well and did I need help. I shook my head, sniveled and said sorry, I was okay, and ran back home. She didn't sing Wagner but she could have, my father said. She was in fact preparing herself for Isolde when she got sick. I was able to listen now without weeping too much, and every morning her voice soared in my ears and I forgot to look at every bench on the way.

Was he still on the streets? Was I looking to save him again? He hadn't let me the first time around. If any saving was done, it had been the other way around. But truth was, it hadn't been about saving at all. He'd been the wedge that widened cracks that had already been there. It had been about something else altogether.

A year ago, Jake had come for his stuff and moved out for good. I hadn't heard from him since, and I didn't miss him. The other day, I was about to throw away The New York Times wedding announcements pages when my eye caught a picture of him holding a girl's hand. He looked happy and thinner. Did she like opera, I wondered. Maybe if I had liked opera sooner, I might have kept him. But of course, it had never been about opera.

Today, as I came back from teaching my class, I found a small envelope in my mailbox in a handwriting I didn't recognize: two tickets for The Juilliard Orchestra performance on February 14th, 2014 at 8 pm in Alice Tully Hall. Sacha Davidov would conduct four world premieres by Juilliard composers. The note said: *"I hope you and your father can come. Matt."*

I was dizzy, the words on the note were fuzzy, I read them again in the elevator. And again. And I was so choked up that I had to sit down the moment I got in. There was no return address. February 14 was a month away. I didn't know how I was going to wait all that time without a clue about what this meant.

When I called him, my father said it was news to him. Of course he would come. Should I call Juilliard, I asked him. He laughed.

I am an old fashioned man, he said, but even I know that you don't need to call Juilliard, you can look it up online and find out quite a lot. You can check their concert series, for example, and see the actual program for February 14th. Question is do you want to or do you want to be surprised? Didn't you use to say you liked surprises?

Yep, I said, it was Jake who hated them.

17

When Mr. Marciano came back, she, Lucie, couldn't believe how sick he looked. All skinny, with a beard so tangled up with things, things that properly didn't belong there, should have been on trees or on plates, these little bits of green and yellow and brown in this thickness of blackish greyish hair, all curly and foreign, and she almost didn't recognize this demented looking man, and she took two steps back until she yelped, YES, it's YOU and ran into his arms and she didn't care that he didn't smell so good, he was back.

I kept your piano, she told him, it's tuned, and I am taking lessons and when I play I think about you every time, and of course you can have it back, we took good care of it me and my mom, and my piano teacher said she'd never heard a piano that sounded so mellow but with keys that made your fingers work hard, which was good when you were learning she said, and she comes here to give me my lessons just so she can play it a little herself, but of course it's yours, and – and – and that's when Lucie burst into tears and he said, here, here, I don't want the piano back, Lucie, it's yours. I gave it to you, it's for forever. And what she didn't ask then is if he was back for forever because she was figuring out right then on the spot that if he disappeared again she didn't want to be prepared because it would ruin this happiness she felt now, deep below her skin.

He'd gotten his old job back, teaching at Juilliard. Music theory and piano. And he moved to a studio on Cranberry Street not far from them.

Why didn't you pick a place near Lincoln Center, she asked him.

Way too expensive out there, and I love Brooklyn Heights, the trees, the river, and besides, you're here, aren't you? And how could I give you all the lessons you need if I live far away.

And he laughed and she thought she should tell him how much she loved him but she couldn't quite because she didn't want to hear that she was too young to know what loving really was. But she knew, see, she knew that when you loved, it was like going full speed, head on against a wall, fast, faster, terrified, and you felt the violence the intensity that burned inside so you could do nothing but go for the destruction of everything that didn't matter, that wasn't related to what you felt, so that you were left only with this thing that ate at you until it burned itself out. She doesn't know how she knows this because she's never felt like this before, but she knows that feeling is everything since it's only what's left when everything is dead, when even love is dead. She knows that's how he felt when he lost his wife, now she understood. She was certain there was no God. She had read about Pascal's bet in one of her mother's books. Lucie, she bet the other way, she bet that God didn't exist. It was fifty-fifty, right? Either He existed or He didn't. She was sure she was right, because if you looked around, you could see that the God hypothesis was dumb, all the

meanness, the wars, the terrorists, the
mindless killings of little kids, the
corruption, the hurricanes, it didn't hold, so
all you had was in the moment, and it had to
be lived as hard as you could, which was
almost impossible when you were fourteen
and your mother was after you all the time
reminding you about homework, curfews,
manners, and you loved your mother
because it had always been just the two of
you, close, together, and Lucie didn't think
there could be anyone else, and she was sure
there wasn't. Until now. So what Lucie
wanted was to be free so she could love
Matt with all her might, and maybe it would

be catchy and he would know that she played for him the best she could possibly play because that's what he wanted from her, and maybe that was enough for him to love her back, even though she was just a kid who didn't know what to do with all her stupid feelings.

18

I wondered what it would be like to be another woman. Not Emma. Someone more normal. More like everybody. Someone with a boyfriend who would stay because if I were that woman I'd know how to keep him, and we might get married and even have kids together. Not too late for kids. And they would look like him or like me or a bit of both and they would go to school and I would cook for them and help with their homework and be there for them, always be there for them, except of course when I taught my classes but they'd be at day care or preschool or something and I'd manage my schedule to be home when they got home, and what the hell was I talking about? Jake and I didn't want children. I had made a big point about that and I bet that now he was going to have a whole passel of them with the pretty blond girl in the picture and they will take them to Nantucket and his parents will be very proud and teach them to ride horses and sail. If I had kids, my father would read them Homer in Greek and they would listen to my mother singing opera and they would turn out to be unlike everyone else and it would start all over again, the feistiness, the unwillingness to settle, and of course the loneliness.

All the men I knew were married or lived with someone. I met them at professional conferences, and I knew how easy it was to take them to bed. They wanted it, they figured it was their time out, their little vacation, no one would know and they'd get back to Sarah or Vicky or Kathleen and bring the kids something back from New Orleans or LA or San Francisco, and they wouldn't know their daddy had himself a little party with someone he'd never see again. And I told myself I was free, I could do what I wanted without guilt. They probably didn't feel guilty, the men, they felt entitled to their parenthesis, something that rewound them a bit and for a little while anyway they were really eager to make love to their wives until the routines set in again.

But in fact, I only tried it once, before I met Jake. We got to this man's room and he took his wedding ring and put it in his pocket and it was such a small pathetic gesture that any excitement I had felt over the drinks, the talking and flirting during dinner and in the elevator, all that desire evaporated, and I left.

When I got home I called Abby, my best friend, who lived in Denver and was a lawyer with the ACLU, and told her. Abby couldn't stop laughing.

I can't believe you're such a nutty romantic, she said, haven't you read what's her name, you know, the woman who wrote *Fear of Flying*?

Yeah, I said, Erica Jong.

So why can't you enjoy a good, meaningless without strings attached? Abby went on.

I didn't have an answer, and, soon after, I met Jake, or rather reconnected with him at some Michigan alumni thing, and then we moved in together.

But it wasn't Jake in my head now. It was another man, one I didn't understand because I knew so little about him, and here I was again with old thoughts and habits that you had to know someone, their pedigree, their CV, all the little boxes to check: white, check; Protestant or Jew, check; educated, check; Harvard or Berkeley, check; as if any of this mattered because even when all the little boxes matched or felt safe, there was no safety.

Safety was a myth, a mirage. And it certainly wasn't what love was about.

*Au contraire.*Matt Marciano was a bomb set to go off in a month. I would not look up Juilliard on line or the concert series.

19

Emma. I saw her ponytail coming out the back of her Barnard cap, the little frizzes plastered on the sides of her face and on the nape of her neck, the wet spot on her back. I heard the sigh when she sat down on my bench the first time, not close, and looked at me, her legs stretched in front of her. I hoped she wasn't going to talk, ask questions. I didn't want conversation. She hadn't, she had just nodded, a quasi-imperceptible nod, and I had nodded back, and stopped thinking about thoughts and closed my eyes. I didn't trust words any more.

Did I now? Maybe sufficiently to work again. To teach Lucie, who thought she was in love with me. She *was* in love with me. The way I loved my piano teacher when I was fifteen. Madame Weil. She had been all angles, but the moment she put her bony hands on the keyboard to sound a line, she became someone else and I was a goner. I had hated myself, my erections, my pimples, my braces, my chubbiness.   She never looked at me, only my hands. She said I had strong piano hands, long fingers. All I needed was to relax. I was too tight all the time. Her voice turned me on, I wanted to stay there and do scales all day if she would just talk me through them, and I worked at home hours and hours, just remembering her breath when she leaned over my shoulder to point out something on the page, *pianissimo,* see there, Matt?

There was something good about this teenage love, this first passion when you gave everything to someone who didn't even knew how you felt. Or if she did, she didn't let on, because letting on would stoke the fires. In fact, it would have scared the shit out of me had there been a hint of reciprocation. So it remained as it should, a rehearsal, a try out, to see if you could come out on the other side of something, and in the meantime you were lost to everyone else, your mother was on your back all the time, because you forgot your coat at school again and walked home in the cold in a bare shirt, and you could catch your death, or you didn't hear when she called you to sit down at dinner, you were still playing the damned scales and having a fantasy about Madame Weil, whose hair was down instead of her usual tight chignon and you had such a hard on you had to get up, and you finally heard the now very impatient voice of your mother yelling for you to come and sit down, food was getting cold. I had to be careful with Lucie.

Emma. It was Emma I thought about. I didn't want to be careful with her. I wanted to tear her clothes off and kiss every single inch of her body, taking my time, and I didn't know how long I could make myself wait.

*   *   *

I had Lucie come to my office at school for a run through of the *Etude* today. I asked Manny to listen and also if he would play the left hand for her and show her how to do the semiquavers, the runs that are so hard to sustain for the entire piece. I had given her recordings of Richter and Horowitz and Rubinstein and asked her to tell me how they differed and which one she preferred. She said Rubinstein. He missed a lot of notes, but he had the right spirit, she said. I loved this kid. She was a natural. She'd make it. She had the spunk and the determination, and she worked hard, harder than I did when I was her age, and she had what no one could teach her, a connection with the music. She intuitively knew how to play it even though she couldn't always execute because her technique wasn't yet fully developed. Another two years and she would have control of her hands.

She walked in, a little bit early and I still had a student with me. I motioned her to sit. I asked my student, Raoul, if he minded and he shot a look at her and said no, fine. She had her partition on her lap and her fingers were moving the whole time. Raoul was a first year student at Julliard, a kid from the Bronx who dreamed of being the next Barenboim. He wanted to give recitals and he wanted to conduct. He was only sixteen. Of course, Mozart had twenty-two works including four symphonies done by age nine and was just getting started. Raoul was working on the last Beethoven sonata, the one Chopin loved and from which he drew some inspiration for the *Etude Révolutionaire*. I watched Lucie when Raoul got to that passage, and she perked up and smiled and I knew she'd heard it.

When Raoul left, Lucie got up and thanked him for letting her stay. He smiled at her, nodded, and walked away. And she looked at him until he was out the door.

20

Something was coming back to me. It was all that listening to the operas every morning when I ran. Images and sounds flooded me. Emma, she was four, and there was this song, soft and sad like a long plaint, but Emma wasn't sad, she held a thin hand, not like her daddy's big hand, but a softer, smaller hand, and she heard the voice of an angel, that's what she thought it was: her mommy, who sometimes came to sing her to sleep, was an angel. She smelled good like a flower. And now her daddy was crying, she'd never seen him cry before, and he took her in his arms and told her that her mommy was gone, she was dead. Where was dead, and when was she coming back, she asked him, because she was used to her mommy coming and going. He said between sobs that she was gone, Emma, she wasn't coming back. Ever? Yes, he said, ever. Why, she didn't like us anymore? Oh no, sweetheart, she loved us and we'll always love her, but she is in a different place now and she can't come back from there. That's what dead means. Do you understand? But Emma thought her mommy had gone flying, that's what dead meant, flying in the sky. She flew and flew and she could see everything from there and it was warm and soft like cotton balls, and really wonderful because now she was light, not like Emma and her daddy, stuck to the ground because they were heavy. Her mommy was all feathery light, but she wasn't a bird. She didn't fly like a bird. She was like a snowflake just before it touched the branch, and because it was the first one, you couldn't ever see it. And now she watched Emma from the tree and she laughed and Emma wanted her daddy to laugh too because it scared her when he cried, and she hadn't done anything wrong, she'd been very good in fact, trying hard to be polite to everyone, all the people who came and talked to her daddy and looked so sad and didn't know what to say to her, so most of them didn't say anything, they just hugged her. Emma didn't like to be hugged by people she didn't know. She didn't want to smell their fear. So she sat on a chair in a corner, smoothed the front of her pretty dress, the one her mommy liked best, the white one with the strawberries on it, and she watched everyone.   She saw her mommy flying around the room. She knew she was the only one who could see her and she smiled for her, because her mommy liked it when Emma smiled and had told her many times that it made her beautiful, and she wanted to be beautiful like her mommy, the angel.

I shook out of the reverie. Did I ever tell my father how I had pictured my mother flying around the house when we were sitting Shiva?

My father had always been here for me. Not much of a cook but we had fun at mealtimes. He'd talk about his day, the classes, the work, his students, and I'd ramble on about my teachers and the kids at school and how silly some of them were. In my four year-old mind I felt my father and I were perfectly happy and he didn't need anyone because he had me. Only last year did he mention a woman he had been seeing occasionally, and I had no idea that all these years, he had tiptoed around me about his own needs and his own life. How could I have held to my solipsistic version of our story so long? Is that why he hadn't shown me the mementos he kept in the safety box at the bank and given me the recordings earlier? Because he thought I wasn't ready?

All these years denying the hole in me, filling it as fast and as best I could with anything, ersatz relationships, work, telling myself how autonomous I was, how I needed no one, how I could take care of myself just fine, thank you, and I made fun of the ditzy girls who wanted to get married with all the trappings, the white dress, the church, how they wanted to be in front of the God they didn't even believe in to hear words that said they were bound to this one for ever, in sickness and in health and all that shit, but they all knew that only one in two marriages endured and what hell break-ups were because they had watched their parents, the separation agreements, the splitting of things, the quarrels over nothing, this vase or that book, what weeks you get the kids, more fights all the time, and I was too smart for that, not for me, I had told myself, all smug, plastering the hole with lies, like if I didn't think about it, it wasn't there. And I covered it up a little more each year, until I sent Jake to hell, and found that the hole was still there and that I wasn't as grown up as I had thought.

21

Two more weeks before the audition. Matt said I was ready but I didn't feel ready. Not after I heard Mr. A. He showed me how to do the left hand and he was so nice about it and I've been doing all the exercises he showed me and my left hand was now moving without my paying attention, like a wound up clock, tick-tocking until its springs are loose again. The trick, Mr. A had said, was to know the notes so well you forgot about them, your left hand knew what to do, scaled up and down as fast and light as you could play it, and you barely touched the keys. The hard part was to keep up the speed and the lightness while you concentrated on the right hand, which was all about the fierceness and the cry, and you wanted to feel that pain all the way until the end. And fiery didn't mean banging on the keys. It was about strength and control so you could be expressive, not loud. All the way to the end, keep the tempo, don't ever stop even if you make a mistake and have to skip some notes. And he had left with a big smile on his round face.

I took the subway home with Matt. It was hard to talk at first because the train was so packed, but after 42nd street we found seats. I should spend as much time practicing as I could until the day before the audition, he said, and then not play anymore just rehearse in my head, until it was time to warm up in the practice room and do a run through with him.

Can *Maman* come, I asked him.

Yes, he said, but she'll have to wait outside with me since no one but the candidate and the judges are allowed in the audition room.

We talked about how I should present the score to the judges, state my name and my age, stand by the piano and announce what I was playing in a clear and loud voice: Chopin, Opus 10, Number 12, *Etude Révolutionnaire*, sit down, make sure I was comfortable with the height and the distance from the keyboard and the pedals, take some deep breaths, relax, and not rush to start.

When you're ready, he said, forget where you are, see the notes in your head, and play. Play for yourself, for the way you want to hear this piece, what it means to you, and your hands will do the work. And remember, whatever happens, don't stop until you're finished.

I wasn't really scared. Maybe it didn't feel real yet. My mother had asked the school to let me come home before lunch so I could practice all afternoon for the two weeks before the audition. And Matt stopped by every night. He said less and less, he just sat and listened. He gave my mother two tickets for a concert in three weeks – the Juilliard Orchestra. He said they'd play his Fugue.

I didn't know you were a composer, I said.

He laughed. I didn't know I was one either, until I did it.

Maybe it would be the same for me, I would play and wouldn't know I could do it until I did it.

*   *   *

It was over. Done. *Fini.* I'd like to say I was fantastic and they were awed, but that was just in my dreams. I didn't stop, I skipped notes and mangled some, but didn't lose the tempo, I played fast enough to feel the urgency. When I introduced the piece, I forgot to say my name, and one of the judges had to ask me. When I was done, they looked grim. They said thank you and I was positive they hated it.

I ran to Matt and burst into tears.

Here, here, he said, you did very nicely. I could hear you were fine. There are still three days of auditions, Lucie, so they won't tell you anything until the end of the week. What do you say we all have dinner and relax before we go home.

They hated it, I said, they looked so mean when I left.

They always do, with everyone, Matt said, they try very hard not to let on and give false hope or any hope at all. Means nothing. I'll pick up your score tomorrow. Now, stop torturing yourself and let's go.

22

I had no doubt they would take her. I heard as much from the president of the jury who was an old friend. But I couldn't tell her that yet. So she still had to wait until tomorrow when the official results would be posted. And I knew how waiting felt, the minutes stretching slowly, your mind getting emptier and nothing you usually did could fill the void: reading, taking a walk, practicing. You couldn't even bear to talk to anyone, as if the thoughts you didn't have were so precious you couldn't bear being interrupted.

I told her about my *Fugue* and how scared I was to hear the orchestra play it, for me to play the piano part, to play a concert again. She looked at me with her big blue eyes.

It's true, I told her.

Are you scared during the rehearsals, she asked.

Yes, I said. Very scared. Remember how you felt before your audition? I asked her.

And before I could add anything she said she knew, it's the same with the *Fugue,* right?

Yes, I said.

I didn't tell her it was about Emma, who for all I knew had forgotten me and was back with the boyfriend. She might not even come to the concert. Or she might come with him, which I guess was worse. It was the first time I had felt something for a woman since Marcy had died. I thought I never would again. We think a lot of things that are not so. When I lost my fingers, I thought I had no life left, no friends, nothing. I was wrong on all counts.

23

Why was this turning into an evening from hell? I was having dinner with my father at *Fiorello* and my father kept telling me to relax. Relax? How in hell could I relax. Would Matt be there? Of course, he'd be there, he was playing, wasn't he? That's why I was terrified. He'd show up and look different, he'd be with a girlfriend, and we'd make small talk, and I'd die. All the reveries of the past year that kept me going would be down the toilet. My father had his Cheshire cat smile pasted on his face.

What's so funny, I asked him.

You, he said.

Well, have your fun, I said.

I was petrified. All I saw was Matt walking away from my building for the last time, watching my life slip away the moment he turned the corner and he was gone with his three bags. I cried then and I still could hear my father's voice. One thing at a time,

Emma, he said. One way or the other, you have to deal with Jake first.

We walked into the Alice Tully Hall lobby a good half hour before the concert. People were milling around already. I held my father's arm while I scanned the small crowd. He wasn't there. I was as disappointed as I was relieved. Of course, he would be back stage. The usher gave us a couple of programs as we walked to our seats: four original pieces by new composers. Matt Marciano's '*Fugue for the Right Hand*' was right after the intermission, to be played by the composer himself. Small write up for each composer next to their picture. *Matt Marciano is an assistant professor of piano and music theory at Juilliard. His Fugue for the Right Hand for piano and orchestra was written in 2012 and is first performed tonight with the Juilliard Orchestra under the direction of Sacha Davidov.*

I heard very little before the intermission. It was like sleeping with your eyes opened and ears closed. I was waiting, I guess. Just waiting.

The lights dimmed again. Matt had short hair and no beard and didn't look like anything I remembered. Yet it was him. The way he strode on stage, slightly stooped, his bow tie impeccably tied. Who had helped him?

He and the conductor bowed. The audience applauded generously. I sat frozen, my hands on my lap, searching for his eyes, and when he straightened up, he looked over the audience as he if were looking for someone. Maybe I was imagining it. He sat at the piano, bowed his head. And there was silence.

He began to play.

Acknowledgments

An earlier version of Part One of this novella has appeared in the February 2012 issue of *The Commonline Journal*, an online literary magazine, under the title *Seven Weeks*.

The sources for the political and news quotes on the 2012 election and Hurricane Sandy are acknowledged in the appropriate chapters.

Thank you to the great team at Harvard Square Editions, who believed in the story, and took infinite care to produce it.

My colleague and friend from Denison University, the late Richard Kraus, inspired me with his elegant short stories and encouraged me to write fiction, as did the late Paul Bennett, poet extraordinaire and one of the kindest men I ever met.

For their good and straightforward advice, always kindly given, I thank my friends Judy Cochran, Henry Copeland, Ira and Karen Fuchs, Susan Garcia, Carole Geithner, Amy and Michael Gordon, Mary Jane McDonald, Axel and Sara Schupf.

For their support and great generosity, I thank Linsey Abrams, Suzanne Gardinier, Myla Goldberg, Kathleen Hill, Mary La Chapelle, Brian Morton, Nelly Reifler, Lucie Rosenthal, Vijay Sheshadri, Barbara Probst Solomon, and Joan Silber, my teachers, friends, and colleagues from the Sarah Lawrence College graduate writing program.

For encouraging me to keep writing, I am grateful to my friend Anna Quindlen, who makes time to read what I send her.

I thank Gail Myers, my former husband and friend extraordinaire, my children Erika and David, and my daughter-in-law Tonya, all of whom remain patient with me when I bug them (have you read it yet?), and keep cheering me on. I thank my French cousin Jean Yves Abecassis who struggles to read my work in English with the help of his dictionary and always sends back insightful comments.

To Walter Mischel, my life partner, my gratitude and love for his spirit and generosity, for putting rejection letters in perspective for me, for feeding me great food when I am still at the computer at dinner time, and for the fun and laughter he brings to my life.

More books from Harvard Square Editions:

Dark Lady of Hollywood, Diane Haithman

Gates of Eden, Charles Degelman

Growing Up White, James P. Stobaugh

Sazzae, JL Morin

Calling the Dead, R.K. Marfurt

Close, Erika Raskin

Living Treasures, Yang Huang

CPSIA information can be obtained at www.ICGtesting.com
Printed in the USA
LVOW01s0958140115

422468LV00005B/6/P

9 780989 596084